Jubal's Christmas Gift

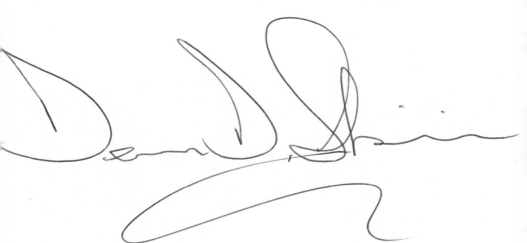

Jubal's Christmas Gift

A Holiday Novella

Dennis D. Skirvin

DEO GRATIAS!
THANKS BE TO GOD!

THANK YOU!

Irma and Herbert Skirvin, (Mom and Pop). May you rest in peace! And thank you, Pop, for your help and guidance with this work all those years ago.

Flossie, my high school sweetheart, loving wife of fifty years, best friend, and partner.

Anthony, Nicole and Alicia, our very special, talented and loving children.

Florence, Anthony and Corky. May you rest in peace!

SPECIAL THANKS

Ms. Robin Hill-Page Glanden, a vibrant spirit whose excellent editing, keen insights, and friendship helped to revive my interest in writing and this book.

Trust in the Lord and do good ...
Psalm 37:3

Table of Contents

VII

CHAPTER I

1979, Late October, the Ludlow Psychiatric Hospital, Wilberton, New Jersey.

"Come on, get movin', you clowns! Hurry it up!" George Schaffer, the lanky attendant in white shouted at a group of male patients as they started down the long hallway. He was escorting them from four o'clock dinner to an outside exercise area.

"If you don't want to go out, it's no skin off my butt."

As George led his charges past two nurses and a volunteer worker, he kept his mouth shut. The patients knew that he was always polite to them whenever the hospital director, or a doctor, nurse, therapist, or anyone else of importance was near. But whenever he was alone with them, George took pleasure in belittling them. "Clown" was his favorite insult. The patients hated it.

"Pick it up, pick it up!" George shouted again. But the diverse group paid him little attention and ambled slowly along. It was their way of needling him back.

When the group stopped at the desk beside the exit doorway, a stocky young guard jotted the time down on a clipboard. He eyed George. "You're late."

"It ain't my fault. These clowns ate too much chow, and now they're sleepwalkin'."

"What is it with you, George? Why are you always calling the patients clowns?"

George smirked. "When you've been around 'em as long as I have, you'll get to know 'em for what they really are, clowns."

Thinking he had put the security man in his place, George demanded, "Come on now. Open the door before I get into trouble."

"Okay, okay," the guard replied. "What's your ward?"

"D."

"How many?"

"Eighteen."

After a confirming head count, he unlocked the door.

"You've got about twenty minutes left," he told the attendant. "You lost the rest of the time on your way here."

As he ushered the patients out, George called back, "Give me a whistle when time's up."

"Will do," the guard said. Standing in the doorway, he counted the men a second time.

Outside in the yard, the men quickly scattered. George stayed by the door and lit a cigarette. "If any of you guys want to smoke, I'll light 'em for you. But if you don't have any smokes, I ain't givin' you any of mine. And remember, when I say it's time to go, that means to butt 'em and hustle back."

Jubal Flowers, a short, portly black man, quietly separated from the other patients and walked slowly to the chain-link fence. For the most part, Jubal liked all the other men in the ward. Two of them, the ones they called "the kids," were in their forties, but most, including Jubal, were over fifty. More than half of the men, like George, were white. The others were mostly blacks and Hispanics, with one East Indian who rarely spoke to anyone.

A chilly wind brought a pleasant medley of street sounds from Wilberton. Jubal gazed down into the town. From a nearby bakery the delicious aroma of freshly made goods caught the wind and rode it to the hospital. Jubal greeted it with a smile.

Two snowflakes flew into his face, and raindrops tapped him on the shoulder. Scratching at his white beard, Jubal noticed the clouds had turned dark and mean. As the wet mixture fell, he thought back to a distant time, and to the incident that first put him in the hospital. He thought about Maggie and their little boy, and the dark, dark day he discovered she had taken him and fled town, leaving him so alone and depressed. What ever happened to them? Where did they go? Now, after so many years, their memory seemed a dream.

2

Jubal's Christmas Gift

The exit door opened, and the guard called down to the attendant, "Couple more minutes, George. Better start roundin' 'em up. We're going to have a storm."

"It's already startin'," George replied. He turned and called to the men, "Let's go! Put out your smokes. It's time to go in, so get movin!"

Most of the men slowly walked towards George but a few grumbled and lagged back, putting out their cigarettes. Suddenly, the rain began falling harder, but it didn't bother the men.

"Come on, you guys!" the attendant yelled. "We're gonna get soaked!" He continued to shout and curse until they finally reached the door.

With a boom of thunder, the rain fell even harder. George pushed through the jam-up at the doorway.

"Damn clowns. They got me all wet!" he cursed again as he shook rainwater from his red hair.

When the patients were all inside and milling about, the guard took a quick head count. "Hey, Schaffer," he said. "You're missing one."

Surprised, the attendant quickly made his own count. "... fifteen, sixteen, seventeen. Damn, you're right. Open the door."

The guard unlocked the door and George rushed back out into the rain. In a moment he spotted the straggler, Jubal Flowers, still standing by the fence. Jubal was gazing into town, and he appeared to be deep in thought.

"Hey, you!" he yelled, "get your sorry butt over here! What the hell are you doing?"

Jubal remained frozen by the fence, oblivious to the shouting as the cold rain continued to fall on him.

George jogged across the grassy yard and angrily yanked Jubal away from the fence, and hustled him back to the building. The guard and patients laughed at the drenched pair as they entered.

"Look who it is!" George cried. "Flowers, Mr. AWOL, the guy who snuck out of here last Christmas Eve."

Jubal stood quietly looking down and dripping rainwater onto the floor.

"What were you doin' out there, Flowers?" George asked him.

Avoiding Schaffer's harsh gaze, Jubal shrugged and continued staring at the floor.

"I hope you're not planning another little unsupervised trip into town."

Jubal suddenly looked up and laughed. "Nothin's gonna stop me this year," he said. "Not you, not them doctors, or that fence out there – nothin'."

The patients all laughed.

"We'll see about that, Flowers," George shouted. "Remember, I have my eye on you. I'll be watchin' you like a hawk. You ain't goin' nowhere — except back to your ward." He took Jubal by the arm and added, "Now let's go! And the rest of you clowns get moving, too."

CHAPTER II

On the same afternoon Jubal Flowers was having his troubles with George Schaffer at the Ludlow Hospital, Stanley Wisniewski boarded a bus for home. The forty-seven-year-old bachelor had had a bad day at the LudMore Rubber plant where he worked. Peering blankly out the window, he thought about the rumors of another cutback at the plant.

Christmas will be here soon, he thought, raking a rough hand through his dark blond hair. *And it always catches me short of cash.*

He had hoped to join the Christmas Club at his credit union as he had done in previous years, but this year money was tight. He worried about the economy, with its high interest rates and inflation, and even higher unemployment. Was a recession coming? Was his job safe? He didn't understand all that was wrong, but then, who did? Even the economists had varied opinions and explanations.

He yanked the overhead cord and the bus pulled over, letting him out for the four-block walk up Hickory Street to his home in Slatetown. *At least I'm still working,* he thought, walking along. *I can always borrow money for Christmas.* He made a mental note to stop at the credit union the next day to see about a loan.

Wilberton residents knew Slatetown by the neat, sparkling-clean, almost identical row homes with their durable, slate-covered rooftops. And Slatetown's residents were just as distinctive. They were mostly middle-class Polish, who stood out by their ethic of hard work, self-reliance, toughness, and resilience. They were the very heart and soul of the community.

As he reached the end of the first block, the intermittent drizzle turned into a hard, steady rain, so Stanley ducked into Zajack's, a favorite neighborhood tavern.

Zajack, the stout owner and chief bartender, called Jack for short, was near the pool table arguing with a man delivering cases of beer on a hand truck. Seeing Stanley, Jack broke off arguing and called out to him.

"Hey, Stan, how ya doin'?" Jack puffed on a cigar hanging between his teeth, while his other trademark, a cowlick, stood up comically at the back of his head. "Be with you in a second, buddy."

Stanley smiled and nodded, and went to the bar, where a few men on stools talked and drank beer. He took a seat, and in a few moments, Jack was back behind the bar.

"What can I get you, Stan?"

"Nothing. I just came in to get out of the rain. I'm on my way home. I've been takin' the bus to save money."

"I know what you mean. It's gettin' tough out there."

Removing his cigar, Jack leaned forward and, looking concerned, asked, "Hey, how's your mother doin'?"

"Not so good."

With a glum expression, Jack whispered, "I'm prayin' for her."

"Thanks."

"How about Stephanie and her two little rascals? Those boys are somethin' else."

"My sister's fine. They're all fine."

Larry, one of the regulars seated by the door held up the daily newspaper and called to the bartender. "Hey, Jack, here's one for you. Says here that, *'Good deeds are investments in the general welfare. Properly made, they will pay dividends for years.'* "

"What's that?" called Jack, looking confused.

Larry explained, "It's a story about some guy named Ludlow, who once lived here in town. It was his favorite saying. It's even engraved on a plaque in City Hall."

"Sure," Jack said, nodding, "Horace T. Ludlow, everyone's heard of him. Hell, Ludlow Street is named after him. He died in the forties, I think, and left millions to charity."

"Ludlow used to own the factory where I work," Stanley spoke up.

"Good deeds my ass," complained Wayne, another regular at the bar. "It's dog eat dog today. Everybody's out to save his own skin. If this Ludlow guy wanted to do a good deed, he shoulda left me some of his money."

"Me too!" called Paul from the pool table.

"If anyone's passing out money, I'll have some too," laughed another patron.

Larry continued. "Down at City Hall the Mayor wants to remove the plaque and put it in storage. But some people are objecting."

"Hell," said Wayne, "they shoulda taken it down a long time ago. Nobody pays any attention to that kinda stuff anyway!"

Paul lowered his cue-stick, saying, "The fat cats are still gettin' fatter and the rest of us suckers are still gettin' poorer. Now they say there's a recession comin'. Who knows! *But* what I do know is that I need another beer. Jack!" He held up his glass for the big man to see.

"Gotcha covered!"

Stanley turned to leave.

"Hey, Stan," said Jack, "you want an umbrella?"

"If you've got one handy," Stanley replied, standing as Jack reached under the bar and pulled out a faded black umbrella and handed it to him.

"You can drop it off next time you come 'round."

"Ok, and thanks. I appreciate the good deed!"

Jack laughed, drawing another beer. "Maybe we'll put that plaque in here. I'll hang it right over the bar." The others, including Stanley, all laughed.

CHAPTER III

Outside on the sidewalk, Stanley suddenly felt a sharp pain in his left leg that caused him to limp. "Darn leg!" he mumbled, knowing the weather had aggravated it.

The leg pain quickly took his thoughts back to Korea and the amphibious landing at Inchon. He recalled the struggle to get ashore, he and his buddies groaning and sweating under heavy packs, the push toward Seoul, the God-awful fighting, and the inescapable feeling that death was coming for him. Lightning bolts of automatic fire caught them by surprise, tearing into them. He could still hear the desperate cries for help. Those cries that echoed in his memory filled him with unending anger and sorrow. Limping homeward, he wondered if these memories would ever fade.

In the 300 block of Hickory Street, Stanley was startled out of his reverie by the sight of his two little nephews, Raymond and Edward, running out from behind Walter Gaska's garages in the next block. A long-time Slatetown resident, Walter was a neighbor and a good friend of the family. He ran a small antique business from his home at 400 Hickory Street, and had a special fondness for the boys, who dashed up onto his cluttered porch and disappeared.

"What are those two up to?" Stanley wondered aloud.

Walking on, he passed the five connecting garages that adjoined Walter's home, where the old man stored his antiques, collectibles and his dilapidated truck. Walter's three-story house was an oddity in the neighborhood. It was practically the only one that was detached.

Reaching Walter's home, Stanley paused to rest his leg. *No wonder the boys like to come here so much,* he thought, as he surveyed the porch. *Where in the world does he get all this junk?*

The porch held a conglomeration of second hand items: old furniture, rusty tools, a half-dozen or so upright vacuum cleaners and more. Looking up, Stanley noted an array of pots, jugs and canvas bags hanging from the ceiling. "It may be junk to me," Stanley chuckled, shaking his head, "but to Walter, it's all special merchandise."

Stanley waded through the clutter to the entrance. When he knocked on the door, one end of the faded ANTIQUES sign hanging on it fell off its hook. He was trying to replace it, when the inside door opened.

"Hello, Stanley," Walter said, with a thick Polish accent. The cold wind blew his disheveled hair about his head. "I thought I heard someone knocking. Come in. How are you?"

"Fine, Walter. How about you?"

"Couldn't be better." The old man smiled.

Stanley stepped inside. He didn't know how old Walter Gaska was or how long he had lived in Slatetown, but he had been here for as long as Stanley could remember.

"What can I do for you?" Walter wanted to know. "Need a good, solid piece of furniture?"

"No thanks. I'm looking for my nephews. They'll have to be coming home for dinner now."

Walter's weathered forehead wrinkled. "Oh, yes. They're here. Come in." He led the way.

Stanley was always pleasantly amazed by the disorder in Walter's home. How could any house hold so much junk? Tables, lamps, bookshelves, beds and other items abounded in the front room – Walter's *best sellers*. Bottles, plates, andirons, picture frames, shutters, and cobwebs filled in the spaces between the larger goods, while a pervasive layer of black dust covered everything.

A narrow pathway ran through the mélange, with numerous smaller veins branching off it, creating a maze. A large wooden desk, cluttered with piles of papers, and a potbelly stove radiating heat stood in the center of the room. The old desk served as the corporate seat of Walter's empire. The stove, smelling of coal, was one of three he used to warm his home.

Passing the stairway, Walter stopped near his desk and said, "The boys were right here a minute ago." Puzzled, he bent over and peered between, around, and over the glut of antiques. "They were helping me look for Zigzag. Now, where could they have gotten to?"

Zigzag was his spry gray cat. He named his pet after the way he made his way through the house.

"Raymond! Edward!" Walter shouted. But there was no answer. "Raymond! Edward!" he called again. "Your uncle's here. He wants you home for dinner."

When the boys still did not answer, Stanley called them himself, in a much louder voice: "Raymond! Edward! Come on, it's time to go home."

Stanley heard a noise upstairs. It was followed by the thud of someone jumping to the floor.

The sounds of footsteps came from overhead, and then, Raymond called down, "Comin', Uncle Stanley." Within seconds he appeared at the top of the stairway and skipped down so rapidly Walter thought he was falling.

"What's the matter, Uncle Stanley?" the dirty-faced, eight-year-old asked. His long blond hair nearly concealed his ears and hung down over his forehead almost to his big blue eyes. He held one hand behind his back, as if he were hiding something.

"Where's Edward?" Stanley asked. "Is he still up there?"

"No, Uncle Stanley. I think he's in the cellar looking for Zigzag."

Stanley frowned. Edward was only six. "I told you to watch out for your little brother. And what are you hiding? Let me see your hand."

Raymond, with a look of guilt, grudgingly complied. He held out a pack of matches, which Stanley quickly snatched from his hand.

"How many times have I told you not to play with matches?" Stanley snapped.

"I didn't light any. Honest!"

"I don't care. The next time I catch you with matches, I'm gonna ground you for ..." Stanley was interrupted by a shout from Edward, who was coming up the cellar steps. "Mr. Gaska, Mr. Gaska!" he called.

Jubal's Christmas Gift

Reaching the small kitchen, the boy called out again, "I didn't find Zigzag. I don't think he's in the cellar. I looked everywhere."

"Edward, get in here right away," Stanley demanded, impatiently.

Edward appeared immediately. He looked like a smaller version of his brother — same blond hair, blue eyes, and round moon face. "I couldn't find Zigzag," he said, "but look!" He waved a miniature American flag. "I found it in the cellar."

The boy was filthy. His hands, face and clothes were covered with black coal dust. Looking him over, Stanley felt his temper rising. He was sure their mother would be furious. But his anger turned to pity as the boy spoke again: "Mr. Gaska, can I have this flag to put on my daddy's grave? I'm goin' there tomorrow with Mommy 'cause I'm gettin' out of school early. The wind blew away the last one I put there. I know my daddy will like it."

"Take the flag, son. It's all yours," Walter said, smiling. "Your father will be proud of you." The old man turned to Stanley, saying, "I'm sorry about the matches and that the boys got so dirty. I'll keep a better eye on them when they come here next time. I bet their mother won't be happy."

"Don't worry about it," Stanley said. "I'll just toss 'em both into the washing machine when we get home." He turned to his nephews. "Now, let's get a move on it! Your mom's going to be worried about you."

The boys were still concerned about Zigzag, and didn't want to leave without finding him.

"Oh don't worry about that old cat," Walter said. "He'll turn up soon. He always does."

With that settled, they all went out onto the front porch. Walter stopped to re-hook his sign while Stanley and the boys continued on, waving back at him from the sidewalk. They hurried up the darkening street through the rain. Near their home, Raymond spoke up, "Uncle Stanley?"

"What is it, Raymond?"

"Do you think we could get new skateboards for Christmas? Our old ones don't work anymore, the wheels are all messed up."

"Well, we'll just have to wait and see what Santa Claus brings this year," he said. "Maybe you'll get them, but not if you don't start listening to me. And that means no more playing with matches."

11

Raymond hung his head.

"You guys know that since your grandmother has been sick there's been a lot of doctor bills, and we don't have much extra money to spend."

"Yeah, we know," the boys sighed.

But then Edward thought of something, and he smiled, saying, "But Santa Claus does! He's got more money than anybody in the whole wide world and more toys, too."

Stanley laughed as they stepped up onto their front porch. "He sure does, Edward." Then, as they went through the door, he thought: *Wouldn't it be something if Santa Claus was also in line at the credit union tomorrow?*

CHAPTER IV

At Ludlow Hospital, Jubal Flowers changed into dry clothes and stood by a window in the ward, watching the rain and snow mixture pelt the hospital grounds. The wind and the snow ...

He remembered it was snowing hard the first time he came to Ludlow, that time long before it was a hospital. In his mind's eye, he saw a much younger version of himself with his wife and small child, trudging past a group of street corner carolers who sang of holiday cheer and good will.

The icy wind cut through them as they made their way unnoticed to the sprawling, hilltop home of Horace T. Ludlow, the wealthiest man in town.

"You're a damn fool, Jubal," his wife shouted. "And I'm a bigger fool for followin' you here in this God-awful weather." She clutched her tattered jacket at the neck, trying to keep the cold out.

"Stop it, Maggie," Jubal snapped back at her. "You're always complainin'. This is gonna work, I tell you.... I've got a good hunch it will."

"You and your hunches!" Maggie shot back, flapping her arms against her sides in a futile attempt to get warm.

At the high gate in the stone wall and fencing that surrounded the grounds, Jubal stopped and stared ahead at the gaily-lit mansion, listening to the sounds of Christmas music. Cheered, he turned and knelt by his son. "You trust me, Billy, don't you?"

"Sure, daddy," the little boy replied, shivering in the cold. *"I trust you."* His wooly black hair was nearly covered with white snow, and little snowflakes clung to his glistening cheeks.

"That's my Billy Boy!" Jubal smiled, hugging him and brushing the snow from his hair and face. *"That's my boy!"*

But when the boy added, *"I'm cold, daddy,"* and started to cry, Maggie exploded.

"See!" she hollered. *"I told you this was crazy. You wanna make a fool of yourself, go ahead, but I've had enough. We ain't stayin' out here any longer. It's too cold."* She grasped their son's arm, turned away and trudged off with him in tow. *"That drafty old shack of ours is lookin' mighty good 'bout now."*

"Good God, Gerty — Maggie!" Jubal shouted. *"Don't go. Have a little faith. Come back here!"* But she ignored his pleas and kept going. Jubal watched them for a while, and when he could no longer hear Billy crying, he turned back to the mansion and walked through the gate. With hopeful expectations, he muttered to himself: *"I sure as heck ain't no fool! ... I've heard a lotta good things about this man, and with this being Christmas Eve.... Heck, you just never know; no, sir, you just never know."*

Jubal smiled when he remembered it all now and how it turned out. He could never forget the great kindness that Mr. Ludlow had done for him. He owed Ludlow a debt of gratitude and he had made up his mind that he would repay it.

Jubal sat down on his bed, opened the top drawer of his nightstand and pulled out a pen and small pad of paper. "How to start?" he murmured, looking toward the window for inspiration. "How to say it?" He glanced back at the blank paper, thinking ... thinking, until it suddenly hit him.

"Got it!" he said with a smile. "Yes, sir, I've got it!" In large, capital letters, he wrote at the top of the paper: I. O. U. Then, while humming a Christmas melody, he continued to write, but he had barely begun when a nurse suddenly came in to the ward, pushing an empty wheelchair.

"You seem very happy, Mr. Flowers," she said, startling him on her way past his bed.

Jubal abruptly pulled his pen back and quit humming.

"What are you writing there?" she asked, stopping at a nearby patient's bed.

Jubal hesitated before replying, "Nothing."

"Well you must be writing something!"

"Nothing important … a letter to Santa," he fibbed.

"Oh, a wish list," the nurse said, good-naturedly. "I hope you get everything you ask for."

Jubal nodded. "So do I."

She turned away to attend to the patient she had come for.

"So do I," he repeated.

In another part of Ludlow hospital, Dr. Julia Nichols took a seat in the front row of a conference room where a group of staff psychiatrists were about to be briefed by the hospital director, Dr. John Stoddard. As her colleagues entered and took their seats, Dr. Nichols tucked a strand of blond hair behind her ear, adjusted her round, tortoiseshell glasses, and scribbled notes onto a clipboard. She didn't mind these informational meetings, but they always seemed to waste so much of her time.

Moments later, Dr. Stoddard came into the room. Everyone sat up in their chairs and looked on attentively. Dr. Nichols fidgeted with her pen as Stoddard sat on the edge of a desk at the front of the room and started his talk.

"I promised you all that I was going to be brief, and I intend to stick to my word. I know you're all busy. But I want to give you a quick heads-up on a policy change concerning our long-term patients. Beginning in the new year, we are going to take a close look at all those patients who have been here for more than five years.

"I am asking you to identify all your patients who fit into this category and to reevaluate their needs and weigh them against the needs of this institution as it copes with a rapidly expanding patient base.

"Now, please don't misunderstand me. We're not going to release any patient who absolutely needs our care. I'm talking about those individuals who could safely function on the outside by themselves or with the initial help of a halfway house. We're targeting those capable patients who over the years have been — well, how should I best put this — those who have been simply warehoused here."

As Stoddard hesitated to draw a breath, a hand went up in the center of the room and a young doctor stood to ask a question. Dr. Nichols raised her clipboard onto her lap and began to jot down the names of some of her patients who fit the criteria as outlined by Stoddard. The name Jubal Flowers was at the very top of her list.

CHAPTER V

"Is that you, Stan?" Stephanie called from the kitchen, as her brother came in the front door of their home at 408 Hickory Street.

"Yes, and I've got the boys with me," he replied, noting the pleasant aroma of golabki coming from the kitchen. The rolled cabbage and hamburger dish was his favorite. It had been his father's, too. "Come in here for a minute. I want you to see something."

With a couple fingers, Stanley gently touched the crucifix hanging on the wall next to the door. His father had brought the sacred icon from Poland in 1939, when the family escaped the Nazis invasion of their homeland. Stanley was just seven-years-old at the time, but he could still recall the terror in his parents' eyes. In heartfelt thanksgiving for their new country and new home, his father hung the crucifix soon after moving in, and it was his habit to touch it whenever he left or returned home. After his father died, Stanley kept up the tradition.

"I'll be right in!" his sister called.

Raymond and Edward made a sudden move for the stairway.

"Oh, no you don't," Stanley said, grabbing them. "You guys are going to stay right here. I want your mother to see you."

They fidgeted and shifted from foot to foot, nervously anticipating their mother's wrath.

Stephanie entered the room smiling. She looked pretty in jeans and a red sweater, but her smile quickly soured when she saw her dirty sons. "Oh, my God! What happened?"

"They were in Walter's place, helping him look for Zigzag," Stanley explained.

"How many times have I told you two not to play in there?" the thirty-three-year-old Stephanie asked. "It's too dark and dirty, and you might get hurt."

"Aw, Mom, how are we gonna get hurt?" Raymond argued. "There's nothing in there but junk and old furniture."

Edward held up the tiny flag. "Look what Mr. Gaska gave me! I'm going to give it to Daddy tomorrow. Uncle Stanley said he'd be real proud of me."

Stephanie knelt and kissed Edward softly on his sooty cheek and took the flag from him. "That was very nice of Mr. Gaska. It's a fine flag, Edward. We're all proud of you, dear."

She hugged him gently. Standing up and changing her tone, she commanded, "Now, go right upstairs and get out of those dirty clothes. Wash up and put your pajamas on. Dinner will be ready in a few minutes."

"But why do we have to wash?" Raymond asked. "Uncle Stanley said he was gonna put us in the washing machine."

As Stephanie looked on smiling, Stanley laughed, "If you guys don't behave, I just might do that. Hey, remember the skateboards. If you want them for Christmas, you'd better be good. Santa Claus is probably watching you right now."

"Okay, Uncle Stanley," Raymond said. "We're going."

They noisily raced for the stairs, but Stanley intercepted them. "Whoa, whoa! Hold your horses! Remember, Mom-mom is in bed. So be quiet. I don't want you to disturb her."

Raymond took his little brother's arm and they tiptoed up.

Stanley watched them go, then stepped back into the center of the small living room. He noticed a few letters laying on the TV and picked them up.

"How's Mom today?" he asked Stephanie.

"About the same, although we talked for a little while this morning. Edward talked with her, too. He loves to help and do things for her. He's so cute."

"I wish I knew what's wrong with her. Just a few months ago she was fine, but now ..." Stanley shrugged.

"She's had so many little things go wrong," Stephanie said. "Her back, her knees, the problem with her stomach. It's been one thing after another. Maybe just old age."

18

"But it's not like Mom to be depressed, to just hole up in bed like this. I think maybe she's giving up. It almost seems like she wants to die."

"Well, we must keep on praying, asking God to pull her out of it. That's about all we can do, Stan."

"Yeah, I guess so," he agreed.

A brown envelope caught his attention and, tearing it open, he asked, "Did we get oil today?"

"Oh, yes. I forgot to tell you. The bill is there with the mail."

Checking it, Stanley's eyebrows arched upward. "Jesus, Mary and Joseph! Look at this — $160.00 for 190 gallons of oil. They must think we have a money tree here! If this gets any worse, we're going to have to start burning coal to keep warm, like Walter does."

Shaking his head in angry disbelief, he threw the mail back onto the TV. "Bills, nothing but bills!"

CHAPTER VI

Still grumbling over the bills and feeling the stress that went along with them, Stanley went to the stairs. "I'm going to go wash up, Stephie. I'll check on Mom and get the boys movin'."

Halfway up the stairs, he heard a loud knock at the front door and stopped.

Stephanie flipped on the porch light and opened the door to see two policemen on the porch. One was Sergeant Tom Watson, an old family friend.

"Hello, Stephie!" said Tom, his ruggedly handsome face breaking into a smile. "Is Stan home from work yet?"

"Yes, he's right here, Tom. Come on in." She opened the door wider and the two policemen stepped in.

Watson had been a good friend of Stanley's since their high school days, and they had served together in Korea.

"Hey, Tom, what's up?" Stanley was smiling broadly as he came back down and greeted his friend in the living room.

"I wanted to see if you're up for a trip to Zajack's tonight. We had an incident a few blocks from here so I thought I'd make a quick stop to ask you."

"What kind of incident?" Stanley wanted to know.

"Liquor store robbery. Lot of people out of work these days, Stan. Things are getting tough."

"I'll say." Stanley shrugged. "So how have you been? Haven't seen you for a while. Looks like you picked up a few pounds." He chuckled, and gave Tom a slight poke in his stomach.

"Been fine, and yeah, Sharon feeds me pretty good, all right. Best thing I ever did was to get married. She tamed my wild streak."

"I'll say," Stanley laughed.

Suddenly, Watson remembered his manners and blurted, "Oh, hell! Excuse me." He turned to the young officer standing by the door holding his hat, and pulled him forward. "This is my new partner, Steve Dixon. He's been with me just over a month now."

The blond nodded. Stanley offered his hand and introduced himself and his sister.

"Nice to meet you both," Dixon said, giving Stanley's hand a firm shake. He smiled at Stephanie. "Tom's told me a lot about you, Stanley. You guys must have been something in Korea."

"That we were." Stanley agreed.

"Steve's a Vietnam veteran," Tom broke in. "He's been on the force a couple years now. I told him a lot about Korea, Stan, but mostly just the good times." The sergeant laughed.

Stephanie's pleasant smile disappeared at the mention of Vietnam. The word chilled her, reminding her of her own personal tragedy, of the time when other uniformed men came to her door with the stunning news of her husband's death.

Just then, Raymond and Edward, scrubbed and pajama-clad, came racing down the stairs. Seeing the policemen, they became excited.

"Hi, Sergeant Watson," they cried. "How are you?"

"Fine, boys! How are you guys?"

"Real good." The brothers looked at Dixon curiously.

"I'm glad to hear that, fellas," the sergeant said. "In case you're wondering, this is my new partner, Steve Dixon."

Dixon smiled and gave the boys a hello.

"Say hi to the officer," Stanley coaxed.

Overcoming their shyness, they said hello and shook hands with the patrolman. Raymond boldly asked him, "Hey, can we see your gun?"

"No, I'm sorry, guys. It's only for emergencies. Know what I mean?"

"Oh, sure, we understand," Raymond replied. "Like a bank robbery or something like that?"

"Right," Dixon said, grinning. An idea suddenly came to him and he knelt on one knee to share it with the boys. "Hey, there is something I can show you guys, though," he said, enthusiastically. "It's a trick I learned a long time ago." Reaching into his pocket, he pulled out a shiny quarter and held it up before the boys. "Watch closely. This quarter is going to vanish right before your eyes."

He closed his hands around the coin, and rubbed them together. "Watch, watch closely!" he said. Raymond and Edward pressed in closer, staring with big eyes.

"Voila!" Dixon cried, opening his hands, showing that the quarter had vanished.

"Holy Mackerel!" Raymond shouted, amazed. "Where did it go?"

"Yeah," Edward said, "where is it?"

With a chuckle, Dixon put his hand up beside Edward's ear and pretended to pull the coin out of it.

"Here it is," he exclaimed with a laugh, holding it up for all to see. "It was in your ear."

"Hey!" Edward cried in surprise, touching his ear. "How did you do that?"

"Yeah," Raymond added, "show us how to do it!"

But before Steve could reply, Tom said, "Not now, Steve, we've got to hit the road." Turning to Stanley, he said, "Stan, we have to leave. So what about Zajack's later tonight? Are you up for a couple beers and a game of pool? We haven't been there in quite a while."

"Yeah sure. Sounds good. I borrowed an umbrella from him earlier today, and I can return it tonight."

"Great. I'll call you later, after I'm off duty."

The sergeant, seeing the boys were still begging Steve to show them how to do the trick, ordered: "Let's go, partner!"

Steve put his cap back on and grinned at the brothers. "Sorry, guys, I gotta go, but I'd be glad to come back sometime and show you some more tricks. The Great Steverino has many more up his sleeve." He looked at Stephanie and smiled.

"Can he, Mom? Can he?" the boys cried.

Stephanie hesitated before answering. "Well, I don't see why not."

"Come on, Steverino!" Tom grabbed his partner by the arm and pulled him towards the door.

"Nice meeting all of you," Steve said. He nodded at Stephanie. "I hope to see you again."

Jubal's Christmas Gift

The family called good-byes and stood at the door waving to the officers as they went out into the rain and got into their patrol car.

After they sped up Hickory Street, Stephanie closed the door and sent the boys into the kitchen to set the table for dinner.

"That Tom!" Stanley laughed, thinking of his friend. "He'll never change. He's a classic."

"He sure is," agreed Stephanie. "I still can't get over him being a policeman, even after all these years. I keep remembering the way he used to take my bicycle from me and ride it up and down Hickory Street." She laughed. "He loved it when I chased after him. He just loved to tease me."

Reflecting on her words, Stanley walked to the stairs. He took a couple steps up, stopped and said, "Yeah, who would of thought he would grow up to be a cop? Crazy old Tom."

"Not me, that's for sure." Stephanie asserted. "His new partner sure was nice to the boys. What did Tom say his name was?"

"Dixon. But I forget his first name."

"Steve!" Stephanie suddenly recalled. "That was it, Steve Dixon, such a nice guy, and handsome, too."

Surprised, Stanley took a half-step down. "You thought he was handsome?"

"Yes, very good looking."

"I thought you had given up noticing men."

Stephanie's smile vanished. Realizing he had upset her, Stanley quickly came down the stairs, put his arms around her and pleaded, "Forgive me, Stephie? I didn't mean to hurt you. It's just that you're so young and so pretty. There's no one more beautiful than you. Really, I mean it."

She wiped a tear from her eye.

"I love you so much, little sister, and the boys, too — like they were my own sons. But it's killing me to see you pining your life away. You should be out dating. And as much as I love Raymond and Edward, they need a real father, with a home for all of you."

The emotional tremor in his voice brought Stephanie to tears again. She tried to speak but couldn't. Then she wiped her eyes and, in a low voice, told him, "I don't want to date anyone." Pulling away from him, she added, "I miss my husband, Stanley. I miss Raymond."

Regaining her composure, she said, "Now hurry upstairs, dinner is almost ready." Quickly she went into the kitchen to check on the boys.

Standing by the doorway, Stanley touched the crucifix and said a quick prayer, asking God to take away his sister's lingering grief and help her find happiness again. Wiping at his eyes, he went upstairs to wash and visit his ailing mother.

CHAPTER VII

Zajack's was smoke-filled and noisy when Stanley entered the tavern. It was unusually crowded for a Thursday night. Carrying the borrowed umbrella, he noted that all the tables were occupied with boisterous patrons, huddled close to pitchers of beer, drinking, eating, smoking and laughing it up.

Stanley sat down at the bar. Within seconds, Sophie, the plump barmaid, greeted him with a gap-toothed grin. "What'll it be, Stan?" He ordered a draft beer, and returned the umbrella. It was 9:15 and Tom Watson was nowhere in sight.

Stanley sat quietly sipping his beer and watching Sophie move behind the bar, filling mugs and ringing up cash. When an argument erupted between her and a young man at the bar, Jack rushed in from the kitchen.

"Okay, pal," Sophie said, steaming out from behind the bar, "you asked for it." With a swipe of a massive arm, she swept aside the young man's defenses, seized him by the collar and the seat of his pants and tossed him out the front door. The room erupted with laughter. Jack returned to the kitchen, leaving a cloud of cigar smoke in his wake. Amidst the uproar, Stanley saw a table open up just as Tom came in.

The two men met at the table and sat down. Sophie quickly appeared for their order. Moments later she was back with a pitcher of beer.

Tom filled their glasses. "Are you up for a game of eight ball?" he said, glancing at the pool table.

"I don't think so," said Stanley, shaking his head. "My leg's been giving me fits today."

"Sorry to hear it. Maybe it's the weather, the cold rain?"

"Who knows?" Stanley shrugged.

Tom thought for a moment. "You know, Stan, I was pretty lucky."

"What do you mean?"

"In Korea — lucky I wasn't wounded."

"We're both lucky we weren't killed," Stanley said.

"Yeah." Tom raised his glass and chuckled, "And lucky Zajack's has plenty of beer."

With little letup the two friends enjoyed rehashing old times, but when talk turned to more recent years, Stanley's mood began to sour.

"Things couldn't be better, Stan, knock on wood," Tom declared, rapping his knuckles on the table. "The kids are grown and taking care of themselves now. The job's going fine. I love police work. But still I'm planning to retire soon. I can draw my pension and work part time. Yeah, things are good. There's a lot to be thankful for."

Noticing Stanley's glum look, he poured another round and continued: "What the heck, you've got a lot to be thankful for, too. If it wasn't for your father, God rest his old Polish soul, bringing you over here to Slatetown, no telling what might have become of you.

"I'm sure things will work out for Stephie sooner or later, and your mother will get better. She's a tough old bird. Remember when we were kids, and she'd throw me out of your house whenever I got too rowdy." Tom laughed at the memory, adding, "She's bound to snap out of it before long."

Stanley forced a grin. "Yeah, I suppose so."

"Hey, you've got a good job, a great family, and you're eating three squares a day. That's a lot better than we had in the war."

Stanley looked away.

"Hey, what's the matter?" Tom asked. "Why so glum all of a sudden? Beer getting to you?"

"No — I was just thinking."

"Yeah?"

"Funny, but I once wanted to be a cop."

"No kidding? What stopped you?"

"My leg! It got pretty messed up in the war. They wouldn't take me."

"You never told me," Tom said, surprised.

Stanley shrugged. "No, I never told a lot of people," he said. "But it's water under the bridge now."

The two turned silent, sipping their beer. Then Stanley opened up again.

"At the plant, we just don't have the work like we used to, or the employees. We once had nearly 1600 men, now we're down to just over 600, and last year they cut out the midnight shift. It's all made me think about what I've done with my life. I don't have anything to fall back on — no college, no trade, nothin'."

"Oh, man!" Tom protested. "What's going on here? Snap out of it, buddy. Start looking at the bright side."

"Yeah, guess I've been feeling a little sorry for myself lately." Stanley forced a smile and looked at the pitcher. "And look, we're runnin' low on beer."

"That's the spirit, Stan." Tom smiled and waved to Sophie to come refill their pitcher.

Early the next morning Stanley gulped a cup of black coffee and took a quick glance at the newspaper before leaving to catch the bus for work. For twenty-four years, he had been working for LudMore Rubber Inc., which manufactured a variety of rubber products, including hoses and gaskets. He started there as a floor man in 1955 after Korea, rehabilitation, and various jobs around town. The work was hard and dirty, but it was steady and the pay was good. Gradually, he worked his way up to become an extruder machine operator. Sometimes he cursed his job, but he was very thankful for it, his union, and the company.

Exiting the bus and walking the last three blocks to the plant, Stanley thought how this once clean and robust section of town had changed, and was now mired in poverty. He remembered his father saying, "You can't blame people who have no hope." And Stanley felt only sympathy towards those who were changing Wilberton. Yet, it grieved him deeply to see his hometown deteriorating.

LudMore Rubber was founded in 1910 by Mr. Horace T. Ludlow and his friend James Oliver Morehead, who suggested abbreviating their names to form the official corporate moniker for the new company. It grew into one of Wilberton's largest industries and occupied a brick building three stories high and an eighth of a mile long. But in 1979, the once bustling factory now seemed empty, since labor-saving advances and rising costs had cut the work force by more than a third.

Entering the building, he went down a wide, dimly lit stairwell and on into a rubber storage area that was cluttered with debris and filthy with black carbon dust. Passing a cluster of idle fork trucks, he heard the hubbub and laughter of men preparing for work in the nearby locker room. Stanley joined them.

"Hey, Stan, how you doin' this morning?" Daryl Brass, the shop steward, shouted at him.

"Okay, Daryl," replied Stanley. "Friday, right?"

"You got it, man," Brass said as he started to leave. "T-G-I-F!"

Stanley laughed. "See you upstairs."

Inside the changing room, beside rows of faded, rusting lockers, less than half of which were in use, about twenty-five fellow workers were changing into gray work uniforms and black safety boots. Two of the men in Stanley's row were having a loud discussion about winning the lottery.

"Hey, come on you guys, quiet down." Stanley said, changing into his work clothes. "It's too early for all that noise — besides you aren't going to win any big jackpot. It's a waste of your money, a pipe dream." But the men ignored him and went on just as loudly.

Chapter VIII

After dressing, Stanley hurried to a nearby service elevator and, along with others, rode it up to the extruder room on the third floor. But instead of finding the workers at their machines, they were all clustered at the far end of the room.

"Hey, what's up?" he asked. "What's going on?"

Stanley recognized men from other work areas in the crowd, which only added to the mystery.

"Some kind of an announcement!" someone said.

"Can't be good," another man said.

"Hope it's not a strike," Stanley said.

He weaved through the crowd of fifty or so men. He saw Daryl Brass up ahead, talking with a half-dozen suited management men, including his foreman Jim Walters. Brass' usually pleasant face was contorted into a frown.

Dominating the conversation was a young bespectacled Southerner, Ashley Davis, who had come to LudMore during the shakeup a few years back, when Morehead's heirs sold the company to a Mid-western conglomerate. The new owners replaced most of the local management executives with out-of-town managers whose watchword was *austerity*. Stanley recalled how Davis and the other new managers wasted no time toughening their attitude towards the employees, and how that strained relations with the union.

To the best of Stanley's recollection, Davis had never come into the extruder room, and as far as he knew, Davis had never even talked with any of the production workers.

Something's really wrong, he thought while vainly struggling to move closer to the front of the pack.

In the mounting suspense, some impatient workers began shouting, whistling, and stomping their feet. Several by Stanley were laughing, enjoying the unexpected free time at company expense. Frustrated and disgusted, Daryl Brass threw up his hands and stepped away from the management group to face his fellow workers.

"Yo, men, give me your attention!" he shouted harshly. The crowd quieted some, but not enough. "Come on, men, knock it off, please. Mr. Davis here has an important announcement to make. You won't be laughing when you hear this."

He waited until the room was totally quiet before going on. "Mr. Davis is going to speak to us for a few moments. You aren't going to like what he has to say but..." He turned, and with a nod, gruffly told Davis, "They're all yours."

The smartly attired manager stepped forward.

"Thank you, Mr. Rash," he said with a faint smile, mispronouncing the shop steward's name. In a loud voice, he continued, "Men, I hate to be the bearer of bad news..."

Before he could say anything more, Jim Walters, the shop foreman, interrupted him, shoving a small wooden crate across the floor. "Here you are, Mr. Davis," Walters said. "You can stand on this."

Davis glared at the foreman, but mounted the crate as Walters withdrew. Fidgeting with his vest, he started anew: "I was about to say that, in life, we are often called upon to do things that are not particularly pleasant. For me, this is certainly one of those occasions. As the saying goes, however, someone has to do it."

Davis, standing firm and erect, with his hand inside his jacket, looked almost Napoleonic. Someone close to Stanley whispered, "Come on, man, just make the damn announcement."

Davis coughed and cleared his throat. "I'm not going to waste time. I'll come straight to the point. The plant is closing down at the end of the year."

For a few seconds, there was complete silence but then, a low, angry rumble filled the room as the full meaning of the announcement became clear. The uproar intensified as many began shouting protests and questions.

"Please, please, quiet down!" Brass shouted, his hands upraised. "Quiet down! There's more. Come on, listen up!"

Gradually, the men stopped yelling and pressed closer to hear Davis' explanation.

"Yes, it's true," Davis said. "After sixty-nine years of operation here in Wilberton, LudMore is closing its doors. There will be no work today, but you will receive full pay for the day anyway. Starting today, and continuing through the weekend, our accounting personnel will be going over the whole plant with a fine-tooth comb for an inventory.

"Final closing will not take place until December 31. That will be our last full day of operation here. We will be open on Monday and you will all be expected to be here at your jobs."

Most of the workers listened quietly, as if in a trance. Stanley, still in semi-shock, didn't hear all that Davis was saying. All he could think about were his mother, Stephanie, the boys, and the twenty-four years of hard work he had put in here. Suddenly, his leg began to ache again.

Davis continued. "All of you men will be eligible for unemployment compensation and later next month there will be some state people in here to sign you up for it. Also, pensions will be honored. Those near retirement age will be given the option of taking lump sum severance pay. There will be more on that later. Your own union people will be able to explain and guide you best on what choice to make."

Davis glanced at his watch and continued. "Oh, yes, there is one other thing. LudMore will continue to pay your medical insurance for a period of two months after our final closing. That means you're all covered until the end of February.

"That's all I have now, but there will be plenty more out on this later. In closing, I would like to add that it has been a pleasure working with all of you. Thank you for your attention."

He stepped off the crate and started to leave, but Burt Munson, a long time employee, called out from the front row, "Mr. Davis! Mr. Davis! I have a question."

Davis, with the other managers, stopped in front of the man. Looking at his watch again, he said, "Make it fast. I have another meeting in a few minutes. What is it?"

"I don't understand. Why are we going out of business?"

"Oh, I'm sorry," Davis grinned. "I guess I didn't fully explain it. LudMore's not exactly closing down. We're just moving operations south and right now all indications are we're going to Texas."

The news caused another noisy stir among the assembly. Munson quickly raised his arms and, after a few moments, managed to restore quiet. "But why?" he persisted. "I don't understand why."

"In a nutshell, it's money. Money rules everything. That's what it boils down to. This plant is a drain on earnings. The cost of doing business here has become too high, seriously damaging our bottom line. In short, we have to move to where conditions are more favorable."

Davis smiled, nodded politely, and hurried away with his managers.

They had hardly left the room when pandemonium erupted. The men stomped their heavy boots against the floor and, with clenched fists raised high, chanted "No, no, no!" They could hardly believe what was happening. Why hadn't they had some warning?

When one of the men threw a wrench against the wall, Daryl Brass stepped up onto the wooden crate, and shouted. "Men, calm down, stay cool!" But ignoring him, they continued to shout and curse. "Stop it, quiet down, please. A riot won't get us anything." Brass continued but the uproar went on for at least another ten minutes, and then slowly died down.

The plant's closing! The words echoed in Stanley's ears, over and over, like rumbling thunder. His worst fear had come true, hitting him like a punch in the stomach. He was still dazed when the crowd fell silent.

"We're going to hold an emergency meeting at 10 a.m. in the union hall," the exhausted shop steward shouted. "I urge everyone to attend. Maybe we'll get some answers."

The angry, disappointed men had many questions for Brass, but he was unable to answer them. "Come to the meeting!" he repeated. "Come to the meeting!"

Today's shift at LudMore had finished before it started. Stanley went back to the basement locker room and changed. On his way up the crowded, noisy stairway, Jim Walters stopped him. The foreman put out his hand and said, "Stan, other than I'm sorry, I hardly know what to say."

Impressed by his sincerity, Stanley shook his hand and said, "I'm not blaming you, Jim. You've been a good foreman. It was the new owners. They betrayed us; they had no loyalty to us or to Wilberton. You heard Davis, it's all about money, profit over people." Stanley paused and Walters nodded. "But really, I'm not blaming anyone but myself," he continued. "I should have seen this coming; I should have done something different with my life."

"It's not your fault," Walters said, "We can't go second guessing our choices in life. Now I've got to run; I'll see you at the meeting, Stan. Good luck."

But Stanley decided to skip the union meeting. He would find out what happened when he got to work on Monday. *Besides*, he thought, *what more can there be? It's all over for us here.*

Filled with worry and uncertainty, he trudged back to Kirk Street and caught the bus for home. Not being at his extruder at this time of the morning added to his apprehension. The embarrassment of losing his job was already setting in. "How am I going to tell Stephanie?" he wondered. Nevertheless, he determined to go straight home and break the bad news to her. But by the time he got off the bus, his resolve had weakened. When he came to Zajack's, he went in.

Chapter IX

S hortly before noon that same morning, unaware of the devastating blow dealt her brother, Stephanie left home with some somber thoughts of her own. She walked to St. Stanislaus School, in Slatetown, and picked up Edward, who was being let out early because of a teachers' meeting.

They passed row-home after row-home and Stephanie noticed that some of them had fallen into disrepair. *It was so much different when Raymond was alive,* she thought. *Like everything else, the neighborhood is changing, too.*

Edward skipped along cheerfully and waved his little flag. When they went past Rowtowski's Bakery, the tantalizing aromas coming from inside made her think back to Christmas Eve, 1971, to a happier time:

The bakery shop was festive with lights and decorations for the holiday and filled with cheerful customers. Additional customers waited patiently in a long line that extended outside in the cold, half way down the block. Inside, Stephanie paid for rye bread and rolls.

"Here you are, Stephie," Mrs. Rowtowski said, handing her the baked goods. "And have a blessed, Merry Christmas."

"You too, Mrs. Rowtowski. Merry Christmas to you and your family."

As Stephanie turned to leave, the little bell on the front door jingled and her husband, Raymond Grabowski, suddenly pushed his way inside looking for her. In his dress green Army uniform, he had just arrived in Slatetown on an unannounced Christmas leave.

Jubal's Christmas Gift

"Raymond!" Stephanie cried. Overjoyed to see him, she dropped her bag and ran into his arms. The two embraced and kissed as the customers looked on approvingly.

"How come you're home? I thought they wouldn't give you a leave?" Excitedly, Stephanie kissed him again.

"I've got new orders, Stephie.... They're sending me to Vietnam, and I have to report back in two weeks. But it's going to be a great Christmas."

Stephanie's smile disappeared. "Vietnam!"

"Ahh, it's nothing to worry about." Holding her tightly, he kissed her again and again. "We're going to have two weeks together."

Stephanie and little Edward walked briskly through the iron gate at the entrance of Saints of Heaven Cemetery and followed a blacktop road over a rise in the terrain. The sounds of traffic from busy Third Street, fronting the cemetery, faded as they went deeper into the interior.

An overloaded dump truck struggled noisily up the slope Stephanie and Edward were now descending, momentarily spoiling the solitude and serenity. Soon, it went by and exited the cemetery, but as if it had been an ill omen of some kind, its passing brought a sudden change in the weather. The afternoon sky turned dark and threatening, and the light wind became colder, sending the fallen leaves scattering in all directions.

"Let's walk faster, Edward," Stephanie said urgently. "Now it looks like it's going to rain."

Almost running, they descended deeper into the cemetery. Edward looked at the rows of grave markers and mausoleums with wide-eyed curiosity, as they hurried past them.

"We're almost there," Stephanie said as they went towards the northeastern corner of the graveyard. "Let's hope the rain holds off."

Suddenly, Edward could see their destination clearly ahead. Ecstatically, he declared, "There it is, Mommy! Look! The flowers we brought last week are still there." Breaking away, he dashed off with his flag. Stephanie watched him run along the road, then down a row of graves to the grassy spot in the corner of the fence where a line of weeping willows ended and the western border of high, green yews began.

Even though this was a large cemetery, it was a very personal place to Stephanie. No matter where she was in town at any particular time, she always judged her position, not by its closeness to home, but by its proximity to Saints of Heaven. Not a single day went by without her thinking of it and her husband.

As she hurried to reach his grave, her hands trembled as the bittersweet memories flooded back. Yet, today there was an odd character about her sadness that made her anxious. Somehow her pain was different.

Soon she reached the grave and with a tear in her eye, she peered over her kneeling son and read the simple epitaph on the white headstone:

Raymond Grabowski, Sr.
1945-1972
Died Serving His Country In The Vietnam War
May His Soul Rest In Peace

Edward planted the flag, and looked around. "See the flag, Mommy? How does it look?"

Kneeling beside him, she touched the flag and gently pushed it a bit deeper into the damp earth atop the grave. "Fine, Edward, just fine," she said, her voice wavering.

"Wow! The wind really blows it," said Edward. "It's too bad Raymond can't see it."

Trembling, Stephanie replied, "You can tell him about it when we get home."

Noticing her tear-filled eyes, the boy smiled and put his arms around her. "What's the matter, Mommy?"

She did not hear him. She was trying to pray, but something within prevented her from focusing her thoughts. Somehow this visit was very different than all the others.

"What's wrong?" Edward cried. Tugging her waist, he jerked her out of the trance.

"Nothing, Edward, I was just thinking, that's all."

"About Daddy?"

"Yes," she said, wiping her eyes with a handkerchief.

"Is that why you're crying?"

"Yes."

"Do you think he sees us here?"

"Yes, I'm sure he does."

"Can he hear us, too?"

"He can if you pray."

The youngster let go of his mother's waist, folded his hands, closed his eyes and silently prayed. Stephanie patted him lovingly on the top of his head.

Edward's earnest praying did not last long. He cried out in angry confusion, "It's not fair!"

"What's not fair?"

"Daddy can hear us, but we can't hear him. It's just not fair. I wish he could talk to us. Don't you?"

Stephanie's eyes teared up again. "Yes, I wish he could talk to us, too."

The weeping willows shuddered as a sudden rush of wind whistled over the gloomy cemetery. The blast of air buffeted the little flag, but it kept on waving. Stephanie clutched her coat and drew it closer around her neck. The tears she had held back gushed forth as the wind lifted the week-old bouquet of flowers off the grave and carried it away.

In a flash, Edward jumped to his feet and chased after it, shouting, "I'll get it! I'll get it!"

Now, alone by the grave, with tears streaming down her cheeks, she remembered her husband's face so clearly she could almost see it. Again, she wondered just how he really had died and if there had been time for him to whisper her name in his last breath. She heard the clickety-clack of a freight train, just beyond the fence, crawling out of Wilberton. The howling wind whipped up the leaves and sent whirlwinds of them soaring over the cemetery.

Edward's complaint echoed in her ears: "It's just not fair. I wish he could talk to us."

Stephanie spoke to her husband. "Oh, Raymond, I miss you so much. I love you. I'll always love you. But the boys need a father and I need to get my life back together. What should I do? What should I do?"

The rush of the wind intensified, and the clatter of the freight train upset her even more as it seemed to be saying, "Let go ... let go ... let go!" over and over like a slow, solemn refrain.

CHAPTER X

In Zajack's, Stanley sat quietly at the bar, brooding over a mug of beer. Two men were busy playing pool, and the TV droned loudly behind the bar with the sounds of a morning game show.

Two other men sat at a table in the room, drinking and talking quietly, while an elderly couple sat at a table arguing in low tones. Aware of Stanley's newest problem, that the LudMore plant was closing, Jack switched through the television channels looking for something interesting.

"Let's see if we can't get something better on," he grumbled. Momentarily, he stopped at a local news program.

Stanley looked up to see a female news anchor, seated erect at her desk and announcing: "We're going live to Wilberton City Hall where workmen have begun the long awaited — and controversial — renovations. Channel 16 reporter, Hunter Clarkson is on the scene."

Stanley, Jack and others in the bar room watched intently as the casually dressed reporter, with microphone in hand, appeared on screen in the forefront of the City Hall construction project. Behind him, workmen in hard hats and standing on scaffolding were busy removing the bronze plaque inscribed with Mr. Ludlow's once celebrated quotation. Yellow hazard tape cordoned off a safe walkway for pedestrians. A small group of orderly protesters was on hand to complain about the city's action.

Looking a bit confused, Clarkson wondered aloud, "Are we on?" He momentarily adjusted his earpiece, and then, suddenly, put his best face forward, looked directly into the camera and said,

"This is Hunter Clarkson, reporting live from Wilberton's stately City Hall building. Behind me workmen have begun the long awaited renovations of the interior. The bronze plaque that has inspired generations of Wilberton residents is headed for the dust bin of city memorabilia."

The cameraman moved off Clarkson for a close-up of the plaque, as the reporter read the inscription. "'Good deeds are investments in the general welfare. Properly made, they will pay dividends for years.' These inspirational words of Horace T. Ludlow, business leader and nationally known philanthropist, are coming down."

Panning back, the cameraman widened the shot, and those in the bar watched as the workmen prepared to lower the plaque. Clarkson pulled two of the protesters into the scene. One was a tall, distinguished looking man with a gray mustache, wearing a neatly tailored dark suit. The other was a much younger gentleman, a handsome African-American, also wearing a suit and tie.

"Here are two local businessmen who are unhappy with the city's decision to remove the plaque." Quickly checking his notes and then referring to the older man, Clarkson went on. "This is Mr. Michael Kirkpatrick, business leader, community activist, and spokesperson for a group of protesters that has assembled here today. He is the owner of the Bernie's Department Store chain, with the main store right here in downtown Wilberton. Mr. Kirkpatrick, your thoughts."

"Let me first say that we applaud Mayor Rocco for the long overdue renovation of City Hall," he began with an air of authority. "However, removing Mr. Ludlow's stirring quotation is a serious error. Mr. Ludlow was a man of genuine good will and compassion, and an inspiration to so many in this town and throughout the country. His life exemplified the sentiment behind his instructive words, which have hung here longer than my entire life of sixty-six years. For the mayor and city to remove them now is disgraceful and a real dishonor to Mr. Ludlow's memory."

Clarkson quickly glanced at his notes, and interrupted, "Now we're going to hear from another protestor. Mr. Mac MacKenzie, you are the current store manager at Bernie's. Isn't that correct, Mr. MacKenzie?"

"Yes, sir, that is correct," the young man said. "And let me just expand a bit on Mr. Kirkpatrick's words by saying, that although

I've only been a resident of Wilberton for just over a year now, I've become a genuine admirer of Mr. Ludlow. I've read and heard a lot about him, his humanitarian work among the poor and homeless, and especially the black community right here in town. So, like Mr. Kirkpatrick, I believe that removing the Ludlow plaque is not only an affront to him, but also an affront to all city residents of goodwill."

Clarkson turned back to Mr. Kirkpatrick, who seemed well pleased with his associate's comments. "But, Mr. Kirkpatrick, there are those who say that Ludlow's words are outdated and out of fashion. How do you respond?"

"Those people are badly mistaken! How can doing good for others ever be considered out of fashion? Mr. Ludlow was a deeply religious man, and his words remind us that doing good for others is a work of mercy the Lord asks us all to do, something we should strive for, something—"

Jack switched off the television set. "We've heard enough about that. I don't think we need to be reminded of good deeds and works of mercy today, right, Stan?"

Looking glum, Stanley replied, "Yeah, they can take that plaque and toss it into the river! That Kirkpatrick guy doesn't know what he's talking about."

Later that fateful day, Stanley finally left Zajack's and went home.

"Stanley," Stephanie cried, "what in the world are you doing home so early? Is everything all right?"

"No," he replied sharply, touching the crucifix on the wall. "Everything's not all right. The plant is closing down at the end of the year and I'll be out of a job. I should have seen it coming. I don't know what we're going to do!" He slumped into his easy chair and stared blankly at the floor.

"Oh no! That's terrible." After recovering from the jolt, she went to him and did her best to console him and lift his spirits.

"We'll be all right," she said. "It's not the end of the world. God will provide."

But Stanley couldn't reply. Instead he thought about the coming Christmas holiday and his family, especially little Raymond and Edward.

Jubal's Christmas Gift

In the following days, Stephanie repeatedly assured her brother that the family would survive the crisis and he would soon find another job. Yet, despite this, and despite the good wishes expressed by friends and neighbors, Stanley knew the road ahead was going to be a rough one. He couldn't help feeling sorry for himself and, at times, he brooded in silence.

Days and weeks passed, and so did most of Stanley's anger at LudMore and the union, but his disappointment with himself remained as strong as ever. At the plant, there was a general slowdown in production, primarily because most of the employees could see no point to working hard.

At Ludlow Hospital, plans to trim the patient population plodded along at bureaucratic speed. Jubal Flowers remained at the top of Dr. Nichols' list.

In Slatetown, the autumn leaves had been replaced by the numbing winds of an early winter. Walter Gaska kept his potbelly stoves burning around the clock to ward off the cold. Zigzag, his cat, never returned home. "Probably froze or found a new home," the old antique dealer surmised.

Chapter XI

D r. Nichols sat behind her office desk sipping coffee and looking over Jubal's records when she heard someone approaching. She looked up to see George Schaffer and Jubal standing in the doorway.

"Excuse me, Doctor Nichols," Schaffer said. "I've brought the patient you asked for. Here's Mr. Flowers."

"Thank you. Come in, Mr. Flowers, and have a seat. I'll be right with you. Schaffer, you might as well wait outside. I won't be too long."

"My pleasure, doctor." With an ingratiating smile, Schaffer nodded and backed out of the doorway into the hall.

Scratching at his beard, Jubal smiled and took a seat in front of Dr. Nichols' cluttered desk. He glanced around the room as she continued to read over his records. Noting the many diplomas adorning the walls, he said, "You sure have a collection of awards, Doc."

Dr. Nichols nodded. After a few moments, she looked up from her papers. "How have you been feeling, Mr. Flowers?"

"Ok," Jubal said. "Been feelin' fine."

"That's good. You understand that you're going to have good periods, and then there will be other times that because of the trauma you suffered all those years ago, you're going to have darker periods. That seems to be your history. Do you understand?"

"Yes, I understand, Doc.

"With the medication I have you on, those dark periods may not be completely eliminated, but when they do occur, they will have far less of an impact on your daily life. Taking your medication is vital. Do you understand that?"

Jubal nodded. "Got it, Doc. But you sure there ain't no other way?"

"I'm sure, Mr. Flowers. There is no other way. You have to take your medicines. Now do you understand that? It's very important."

"Yes," Jubal conceded. "I understand. I have to take my pills!"

"That's correct," Dr. Nichols said. "You have to take your medicines, which, unfortunately, you have a spotty history of doing and which keeps bringing you back to this hospital."

The doctor paused for a few moments, before beginning again. "Your records indicate that you've been here, on and off again, for more than ten years."

"Sounds 'bout right," Jubal agreed. "I guess if you have to be in a hospital, this one's okay." And after thinking a bit, he quickly added, "The food could be better."

"Other than the food, I'd say you're quite happy here. Is that correct?"

"That'd be one way of lookin' at it, I suppose. But to tell the truth, I don't have no other place to go. Bein' outside durin' the warm weather ain't so bad. But winters, now they can be rough on an old man like me. Too cold!"

"I see your point," Dr. Nichols said, "but by looking at your admission and discharge records, there seems to be a preponderance of October or November admissions. You haven't spent too many winters on the *outside* as you put it." She winked at him.

"Guess that's right," Jubal chuckled. "But why are you tellin' me all this, Doc? What are you gettin' at?"

"I have some good news for you," she said, smiling cordially. "I am going to discharge you."

Jubal sat up in surprise. "Good God, Gerty! Discharge me?"

"Yes, Mr. Flowers. We're going to discharge you. I believe you're ready to return to society. In fact, I feel you're overdue. You seem fully recovered."

Jubal chuckled and scratched his beard. "Well I'll be go to heaven. Ain't this somethin'. Fully recovered! Heck, Doc, I guess

I've been fully recovered for some time now. I just never let on or clamored to get out of here."

Dr. Nichols leaned forward. "And why did you do that?"

Jubal grinned. "Like I said, I didn't have any other place to go. I got no family to speak of, and all my friends are right here in Ludlow. So I thought I'd just stay here."

"I suppose I can't fault you for that. But it's time for you to move on with your life. You can make new friends outside."

"Sure I can. But the ones here are special. They're not like them people beyond the fence. Hey, when am I leaving?"

"As soon as we can get everything in order. Not for a few weeks, maybe a month or so. I just wanted to let you know now so you'd have some time to get yourself prepared. In the meantime, I'm going to assign a social worker to you to help with the transition. Since you have no family that you could stay with, I'm recommending that you be placed in a halfway house where you'll be monitored, then eventually released altogether."

Jubal sat quietly contemplating the unexpected news.

"Is there anything you'd like to say? Do you have any questions or concerns?"

"Will I be out before Christmas?"

"It's possible, but as I said, it's going to take some time. Anything else?

Disappointed, Jubal shook his head.

"Are you sure there's nothing else?"

"No ... except that I'd like to be discharged by Christmas Eve."

"Any special reason?"

"No, just something I'd like to do, that's all."

"I suppose it's possible, but we'll just have to wait and see. Now is there anything else?"

"No, but thank you for always being so kind to me."

Doctor Nichols smiled. "Well, you're certainly welcome, Mr. Flowers. With the exception of your 'unauthorized excursion' into town last year, you've been a model patient. I've thoroughly enjoyed being your doctor. I wish you the best of luck and every success. You will be fine. In fact, knowing you, society will be all the better for having you back."

"Thank you, doc. That's very nice of you to say. Now is that all?"

"Yes. You can go."

Jubal got up and started for the door. Just then Dr. Nichols thought of something.

"Oh, by the way – why do you want to be out by Christmas Eve? Are you planning something?"

Jubal grinned. "No … It's nothing important."

Doctor Nichols came out from behind her desk and took him by the arm. "Is there something about Christmas you want to tell me?"

The old man thought for a moment before replying. "Just that it's the best time of the year. But here recently, the Christ child's birthday has come to remind me of a debt I need to repay."

"Is it money you need?"

"No, it ain't that kinda debt."

"Oh, I see. Well, perhaps you'd like to tell me more?"

Jubal shook his head. "No."

"All right then, Mr. Flowers. But remember, if you decide you'd like to talk about it, my door's always open."

Dr. Nichols glanced at the wall clock, and then called to George Schaffer, who was half-asleep on a nearby bench in the hallway. Soon the attendant and patient were on their way back to the ward. For a few moments, Dr. Nichols watched them go.

Once they were out of earshot, George Schaffer spoke to Jubal. "Remember, Flowers, I'm keeping a close watch on your sorry butt. There isn't going to be any waltzing out of here this year. Got it?"

Jubal chuckled, which only angered George.

"Damn clowns!"

Days later, with clipboard in hand, social worker Rosa DiJulian stepped into Ward D looking for Jubal. But not seeing him, she stopped by his bed to survey his area for a few moments. It was a professional habit of hers, and often provided a further insight into a patient. She noticed a Bible lying on his bed, with a bookmark protruding from its pages, and on the bedside table were a wooden pedestal cross and an American flag.

"No family photos," she said to herself.

On the wall behind the table, a full-year calendar caught her eye. The date December 24 was circled in pencil, and next to it a scribbled notation, the only one showing on the calendar. Curious, Rosa leaned closer to read the words: *Christmas Gift*.

"Hmmm, wonder what that's about?" she said before leaving the ward.

Rosa found Jubal in the day room, seated comfortably on a leather couch in front of a large television set. She took a seat next to Jubal and introduced herself.

"Nice to meet you," Jubal said. "You have a nice smile."

"Why thank you." Rosa said, blushing at the compliment. "Doctor Nichols has told me of your pending discharge and asked me to see you."

"Will I be out for Christmas?" Jubal abruptly asked.

"I'll see what I can do," she said. "Now, I understand you have no family, correct?"

"That's right," Jubal said, with a noticeable tinge of sadness. "I had one once, but ..." He shrugged, and left the thought unfinished.

"Well," Rosa went on, "we'll have to find you a spot in a halfway facility before your discharge can be completed. Space is limited and the wait can often take some time. But I'll try my best, Mr. Flowers."

"That's good enough for me," he said, his spirits rising. "And I thank you kindly."

Rosa nodded, and made a note of Jubal's request.

"Yes sir, you sure got a pretty smile," he repeated.

CHAPTER XII

Nattily attired in a dark suit, crisp white shirt and striped tie, Mr. Charles Greenway, Personnel Manager at Martin's Quality Automobiles, one of Wilberton's premier auto sales establishments, sat behind his mahogany desk and picked up a job application. He was looking it over when a secretary showed Stanley Wisniewski into his office.

"Ah, Mr. Wisniewski, come in and take a seat."

After shaking Greenway's hand, Stanley quickly sat across from him, feeling the muscles at the back of his neck tightening.

"I was just looking over your application," Greenway said, sounding very official. "Everything looks to be in order.... I see that you worked at LudMore Rubber and, other than a stint in the service, that seems to sum up your employment history."

Stanley shifted uncomfortably in his chair. "I started at LudMore soon after getting out of the service. That was twenty-four years ago. Actually, I'm still working there. The plant's not closing until the end of the year."

The man looked up from the application. "Oh, so you wouldn't be available until then?"

"I have a family depending on me, Mr. Greenway. I need a full-time job with benefits. I'll start right now if I have to."

Greenway nodded and looked back at the application. "Of course.... Now, tell me, have you had *any* sort of prior experience in sales?"

Stanley felt a drop of sweat trickle down his back, as he replied, "No, but I'm a quick learner. I'm not too old to learn anything."

After a brief hesitation, the man asked, "And how old are you?"

"I'm forty-seven. Is that a problem?

Greenway fidgeted with the application. "Oh no!" he assured Stanley. "Not in the least. Selling luxury cars, however, can be surprisingly demanding in a lot of ways. Most of our sales force is considerably younger, but no, your age is definitely not a problem. Not at all."

Greenway smiled and suddenly stood up, extending his hand to Stanley, who was surprised and disappointed that the interview was over so quickly.

"Thank you so much for coming in, Mr. Wisniewski. It was a pleasure to meet you. We have a lot of applications to look over, but we'll be sure to give yours serious consideration. Thanks again. You can show yourself out."

Greenway sat back down and put Stanley's application aside, while Stanley left the office, knowing he would never hear from him again, and his job search would have to continue.

In heavy jackets and hats, Raymond and Edward Grabowski sat side by side on the top step of Walter Gaska's front porch checking over their Christmas lists. A lightly falling snow had painted over Slatetown with broad, generous strokes, rendering everything beautifully white and pristine.

"Uncle Stanley said we shouldn't expect much for Christmas," Raymond said, holding up his list.

"Yeah, I know," Edward agreed, looking sadly at his own.

"Guess we won't get new skateboards."

Edward shook his head doubtfully. "No, or most of the other stuff we've asked for."

The two fell silent. To their sudden surprise, the door opened behind them and Mr. Gaska poked his head out. "What are you two doin' out there?"

"We're lookin' at our Christmas lists," Raymond spoke up.

"Yeah," Edward added, "Uncle Stanley told us that Santa Claus was broke this year. And he might not even stop in Slatetown."

Gaska knew full well the trouble the family was having. "Well, there are a lot of people broke this year, boys. Santa's just one of 'em. I heard he doesn't have as many toys to go around. But I'll bet he still stops here, even if it's a quick one."

"You think so?" Edward asked.

"Sure."

"I hope so," said Raymond.

"Here's a suggestion, boys. Why don't you come in out of the cold and together we'll go over those lists of yours? If we can shorten 'em up some, then Santa will have more toys to go around."

The boys frowned.

"We're already not asking for that much," Raymond said.

"Not as much as last year," Edward pointed out.

Gaska thought for a moment. "Well I hear what you are saying, boys. But remember what your uncle said, Santa's broke this year, and he can't afford as many gifts. So the less you guys ask for, the more he'll have to give to other kids."

"Yeah, I guess so," Raymond said.

"It's what Christmas is about, fellas. Doin' good and sacrificing for others."

The boys looked at each other for a moment, and then quickly got up. Gaska held the door open for them. "Come on in," he said. But just as they were about to step inside, he thought of something. "Whoa, wait a second."

The boys stopped in their tracks.

"Raymond," said the old man, "I hope you don't have any matches with you?"

Looking guilty, Raymond lowered his head.

"Give 'em here, son!"

Raymond reached into his coat pocket, pulled out a pack of matches and handed it to Mr. Gaska. "I wasn't going to light any. Honest."

"You better not. If your uncle catches you with matches again, you can forget about any Christmas presents."

"Sorry, Mr. Gaska. You're not going to tell him are you?"

"No, not this time. But if it happens again, I will."

After Raymond said he was done with matches forever, Gaska smiled and patted the boy on the shoulder. "That's a boy."

"Did Zigzag come home yet?" Edward wanted to know as he and Raymond entered the home.

At the mention of his cat, Gaska quickly ran his eyes up and down the block. "No, I'm afraid not. But he's done this before. I suspect he'll find his way home someday.... Now come on, let's get to those Christmas lists."

Tom Watson and Steve Dixon were cruising town in their patrol car on a cold, blustery mid-December evening when Tom suddenly remembered something.

"Hey, Steve, I've been meaning to ask you, did you ever go back and do more magic tricks for my buddy Stan's two little nephews? Do you remember what I'm talking about?"

"Sure I remember. Raymond and Edward, right? The two brothers."

"Yeah, that's them."

"No, sorry to say, I never went back."

"That's too bad."

"Funny you asked though, because I've been thinking about them, and their mother, Stephie."

"She's one sweet kid; they don't come any better."

"I'm sure."

"It was a real tragedy about her husband. He died in Vietnam, in '72, in an ambush. Damn war! She took it really hard."

Dixon shook his head. "That whole war was a tragedy!" he added. "It messed up a lot of people. Left a lot of scars." He stared out his side window.

"I'm sure ... but every war is a tragedy," Tom said, pulling into the parking lot of his favorite coffee shop. "I need a jolt of caffeine. What do you say?"

"Yeah, sure. I could go for some coffee. You know, I started to call Stephie two or three times, but each time I hung up. I really felt for her and her boys. I mean it." He fell silent for a few moments, and then added, "You know, Tom, when I came home from Vietnam, I had a lot of guilt about making it out alive. Survivor's guilt they call it. I'm sure you know about that."

Tom nodded. "Oh, yeah."

"It's hard to explain," Dixon went on, "but that night we were at Stephie's house, I felt it again. The fact that I got out of 'Nam alive, must have reminded her of her loss. It might sound crazy, but maybe she resents me for surviving."

"No way, Steve," Tom replied in surprise. "You're way off on this one, partner. Believe me. You don't know Stephie as well as I do."

"No," replied Dixon, "no, I guess I don't." He broke into a half smile. "But I think I'd like to get to know her."

CHAPTER XIII

By the arrival of Christmas Eve, Stanley had had no luck landing a job. Predictions of a recession and higher unemployment made the outlook for the coming year even bleaker. Soon he would be out of work and there would be a desk full of bills to deal with.

Stephanie did her best to keep the spirit of Christmas alive. By careful thrift, she had saved enough money to buy a big ham and six rings of Stanley's favorite kielbasa for the holiday. She had fresh rye bread from Rowtowski's and she had made potato salad and baked plenty of cookies. *This Christmas,* she thought, *is going to turn out just fine.*

Stanley, on the other hand, felt as if he was carrying the weight of the world. For the first time in his life, he appeared untouched by the spirit of Christmas.

Late that afternoon, Stephanie, Raymond and Edward were putting the final decorations on the tree when the boys began arguing about whose turn it was to place the angel on top of the tree.

"Stop the fighting," Stephanie demanded, stepping between them. "I'll settle it. We'll toss a coin and the winner will do it."

The boys agreed. Raymond chose heads, Edward tails.

Stephanie tossed the coin into the air and caught it on the way down. Raymond and Edward crowded in close.

Stephanie took her hand away to uncover the coin. "Tails it is!" she announced with a smile. "Edward, you win. Sorry, Raymond."

While Edward jumped with glee, Raymond complained, "It's not fair; it's not fair."

Stephanie gave the loser a hug and a kiss. "No, it was fair," she disagreed. "You can't win all the time. But since you lost, you can hang the mistletoe by the kitchen."

Raymond's sour look quickly changed into a bright smile. He turned and ran for the kitchen. Stephanie laughed, then hoisted Edward up into her arms and moved closer to the tree, where he proudly placed the angel onto the very top of it.

Raymond hung the mistletoe with a smile. He jumped down from the step stool and looked up to check his work. Next he turned and admired all the other decorations and ornaments they had put up. "It really looks like Christmas in here, Mom."

"It sure does, and you boys deserve all the credit. You did most of the work."

"Do you think Uncle Stanley will like the tree and all?" Raymond asked.

"I'm sure he will. And that reminds me, I better check on dinner. He'll be coming in from work any minute."

Raymond put the step stool away while Edward followed his mother into the kitchen. "Everything smells so good," he said, taking in a deep breath. With excited eyes, he peered into the oven as Stephanie opened the door to check the ham.

With Raymond at his side, Edward told Stephanie, "I think it's going to be a great Christmas, Mom, even if we don't get any presents."

"Yeah, I think so too," Raymond agreed.

Stephanie felt so proud of her boys.

Christmas Eve found Mr. Michael Kirkpatrick in a joyful, holiday mood. In spite of the poor economic conditions, sales at his downtown department store were much better than he had expected.

Sitting at his office desk, he pressed the intercom to speak with his secretary. "Maisy!" he said sharply.

"Yes, Mr. Kirkpatrick," the woman replied.

53

"If you're not too busy, I'd like to see you in my office for a minute or so."

"Be right in."

In no time Maisy Cunningham came hustling in to his office, looking quite serious. "What is it?" she asked.

Smiling, Kirkpatrick asked her to have a seat, and she sat down in the chair next to his desk.

"Maisy," he began, "how long have you been with us? Twenty-five years?"

"Thirty," she proclaimed proudly, straightening her blue skirt and folding her hands onto her lap. "Remember we had a big celebration back in May."

"Oh that's right," he said, embarrassed. "How could I forget?"

"Well, I wanted to speak with you a bit before you left for the holiday. I want to thank you for your loyal service over all these years. You've been much more than a secretary here, much more, and I just wanted to say that today, and also wish you a very Merry Christmas."

Maisy's big, round face lit up like the sun. "Why thank you, sir. That's very kind of you to say."

"It's the truth," he said, handing her an envelope. "And here, I want you to have this special Christmas bonus."

Maisy took the envelope.

"Go ahead and open it."

Still smiling, she quickly opened it and peeked in at a check made out to her. "Oh my, Mr. Kirkpatrick!" she gasped. "I don't know what to say ... other than thank you, thank you so much. This really is special!"

"You deserve it. I honestly don't think I could run things without you. Thank you, Maisy!"

Overjoyed, she replied, "You're welcome, so very welcome."

For the next ten minutes or so, they sat reminiscing about *the good old days* and so many joyous Christmases. And when she finally got up to leave, he said, "Before you go home, could you please ask Mac to stop by my office."

"Yes, Mr. Kirkpatrick, I'll do that right now. And Merry Christmas, sir, Merry Christmas." Before leaving his office, she suddenly stopped and added, "Oh, and good luck with your meeting with Mayor Rocco."

Jubal's Christmas Gift

"Thank you, Maisy."

"It's a shame about that plaque, sir."

"Yes, it is, a real shame."

Chapter XIV

It was nearly a half an hour later when Mr. MacKenzie, the store manager, knocked at Mr. Kirkpatrick's office door. With the early closing for the holiday, Maisy had already gone home, and most of the other employees had left, too.

"Come in, Mac," Kirkpatrick called, looking up from a spread of papers on his desk. His young associate stepped in with a smile and a vigorous stride.

"Ms. Cunningham said you wanted to see me, sir."

"Yes, that's right, Mac. Have a seat, and give me a moment." He quickly organized the papers into three separate piles, and set them aside.

"There, no more work today," he said, sounding relieved. "From now on, it's all about Christmas!" Reaching in to a desk drawer, he took out an envelope and handed it to Mac. "Normally," he went on, "it's not our policy to give Christmas bonuses to those who've been here at the Wilberton store for less than three years. But your transferring in from Pittsburg to take over management here has worked out exceedingly well. You are a real asset to our company, Mac, and I want you to know how much I appreciate your great work, and your friendship."

"Thank you, Mr. Kirkpatrick," the manager said, smiling, "I sure appreciate hearing that."

"I mean it, everything I've said! Now, go on and open it. Go on."

Mac quickly opened the envelope, and was every bit as surprised as Maisy Cunnigham had been earlier.

"Whoa, thank you, sir," Mac said, looking at the enclosed check. "Thank you very much."

"You're welcome!" Kirkpatrick nodded. "As I said, your coming here has worked out exceedingly well, most especially in this year of economic difficulties."

The two men went on chatting for a short while, until Mr. Kirkpatrick stood up and said that he had to be going. "I have an appointment with Mayor Rocco," he said. "I'm going to give that dunderhead a real piece of my mind, and demand that he put the Ludlow plaque back up on display. I still can't believe he took it down."

"And neither can I," Mac said, with a grimace and a shake of his head. "Especially in this crazy world of ours today."

"Precisely!" Kirkpatrick said, taking his overcoat from a closet. Suddenly an idea occurred to him. "By the way, you're not working late tonight are you?" he asked.

"Yes, I have a few things...."

"On Christmas Eve!" Kirkpatrick protested, waving his hand. "No, no, you simply can't work tonight. I won't allow it." He glanced at his wristwatch. "Besides the store's closed now for the holiday. I've got a better idea. How would you like to go with me to see the mayor?"

Mac smiled. "Sure, I'd love to. We did the interview together, so we might as well shake up the mayor together, too," he laughed.

"That's the spirit," Kirkpatrick chuckled. "Get your coat and I'll meet you in the lobby."

Mac got up. "Better give me ten minutes, sir. I've got a couple things to button up before I leave. I want to see the night watchman, too. I won't be long." He hastened to the door.

"That's fine. See you in ten."

Before Mac went out, he thanked Mr. Kirkpatrick once again for his generosity.

The two men caught a taxi, and instructed the cabby to take them to City Hall. They sat in the back seat passing the time with talk of Christmas.

"It's my favorite time of year," Kirkpatrick admitted. "I just love all the excitement, the hustle and bustle and the goodwill. Not

to mention December is our biggest sales month in the entire year."
Kirkpatrick laughed.

"I can understand you loving that!" Mac chuckled.

"Yes, well that's all true," Kirkpatrick said, turning serious
again, "but it's more than that, much more."

The two men fell silent, each reflecting on his own recollections
of past Christmases.

After a while, Kirkpatrick broke the silence. "Being from out of
town, Mac, I suspect you don't have any family here in
Wilberton."

"Yes, that's right, sir," he said.

"Must be a little lonely for you."

Mac shrugged.

Kirkpatrick thought for a few moments, then said, "I've got it,
the perfect cure: you can come and spend Christmas with my
family and me. My wife Bernadette is a great cook. Bernie makes
an excellent turkey, and even though we Kirkpatricks can get a
little boisterous on the holiday, it's all great fun."

"Oh, I don't know. I wouldn't want to impose on you and your
family."

"Nonsense. Don't be silly. It's no imposition at all!"

The two continued to discuss the invitation, until Mac finally
accepted.

"Splendid," the storeowner laughed. "You won't regret it young
man, believe me you won't."

Moments later the taxi driver pulled over and stopped in front of
a block-wide, neoclassical style limestone building. "City Hall!"
the cabby announced. Quickly paying the fare, the two wished the
driver a "very Merry Christmas." They climbed the stone staircase
leading up to the columned entrance. Once inside the sprawling
lobby, they found the elevator and rode it to the top floor.

"It's this way," Kirkpatrick said, on emerging. He led Mac
through a hall and past a circular balcony that offered a panoramic
view of the first floor lobby where they had come in. On finding
the mayor's office, they went right in.

An attractive, young black woman, the mayor's receptionist, sat
at a desk, talking on the telephone as they came in. Seeing them,
she flashed a big smile and raised a well-manicured index finger,
as if to say, *I'll be with you in a minute.* She ended her call quickly.

"Sorry, gentlemen," she said. "Now what can I do for you?"

"My name is Michael Kirkpatrick and this is my associate, Mr. MacKenzie. We have an appointment with the mayor."

"Oh, you're Mr. Kirkpatrick," she said, as if she had been well informed about him. Looking down, she checked her appointment book. "Yes, I see, you have an appointment, the last one of the day." Her pleasant smile suddenly vanished. "I'm so sorry, Mr. Kirkpatrick, but Mayor Rocco has been called away on urgent business. In fact he just left, and I'm afraid he won't be back until after the holiday. He extends his regrets." Then smiling again, she added, "He asked me to be sure to wish you a very merry Christmas."

Red-faced with anger, Kirkpatrick snapped, "Urgent business my foot! He can't keep avoiding me. Sooner or later, he has to hear me out."

"I understand, sir. Truly I do. I know you're disappointed, and I do apologize. Would you like to talk with his personal secretary? She's still here."

"No," he declined. "That won't do. The mayor's going to hear from me in person, face to face." He pulled away from the desk, saying, "Come on, Mac. We're wasting our time here."

Mac gave the woman a friendly nod and a half-smile, as if to convey acceptance of her apology. Then, quickly he turned and followed his boss out into the hallway.

"I should have guessed it," Kirkpatrick complained, heading for the elevator. "The coward!"

Suddenly the office door swung open, and the receptionist hurried out after them, her high heels clicking on the polished terrazzo floor. "Mr. Kirkpatrick!" she called. "Mr. Kirkpatrick!"

The two men stopped and turned about.

"Oh, Mr. Kirkpatrick, just one minute," she said approaching them.

"What is it?" he said sharply, the irritation still noticeable in his voice.

Before answering, she carefully looked about, making certain that no one would hear. "I know why you came, sir," she began, "and I just wanted to say that I completely agree with you. He never should have taken that plaque down. That was just plain dumb."

Pleasantly surprised, Kirkpatrick chuckled. "Well, thank you, Miss. I couldn't agree with you more."

"And neither could I, Miss ..." Mac added with a grin.

"Beverly Swanson. And here's my card." Smiling pleasantly, she handed it to Mac. "I don't know if I can be of any help in getting that plaque put back where it belongs, but if you think of anything, please call me. I'd love to help you."

"That's very kind of you, Ms. Swanson," Kirkpatrick said. "The battle's not over yet, young lady!"

"No, not by a long shot," Mac added.

"Merry Christmas to you both," she said. "And good luck."

The men wished her a Merry Christmas too, and thanked her once more for her support. Getting back into the elevator, Mac looked closer at her card. Smiling, he put it safely in his coat pocket.

Chapter XV

At Ludlow Hospital, the normal working staff had been reduced to a skeleton force for Christmas. Most of the doctors, nurses and other employees were home sharing Christmas Eve with their loved ones. The patients who were allowed to go home had also left. Unfortunately for Jubal Flowers, Rosa DiJulian's efforts to place him in a halfway house before the holiday proved fruitless. George Schaffer wished he could be off too, but since he had to work, he decided, "What the hell, it's just another night."

Leading a group of patients back to their ward from supper, George made sure Jubal walked near him so he could keep an eye on him. He took the men up a long carpeted hall, passing doors and windows decorated with holiday wreaths and ornaments. Unexpectedly, a door opened in their path, startling him, and almost striking some of the men.

"Hey, look out!" George shouted at the two orderlies who came out into the hall. "What's the matter with you guys? You scared the hell out of these clowns."

With a quick apology, the orderlies walked off. George glared at them as they went around the patients and disappeared down the hall. When he turned back around, he was shocked to see Dr. Nichols standing right in front of him. Jubal watched these developments and slowly edged to the rear of the group.

"Is that the way you normally refer to our patients?" Dr. Nichols angrily asked.

Caught off guard, George stammered. "Why, why no, Doctor Nichols. It's just that those orderlies... "

Taking him by the arm, she led him a short distance away from his charges. "Schaffer," she resumed in a low, angry tone, "I don't care what your excuse is. No one is going to talk like that to our patients. If I ever hear you do that again, I'll have you thrown out of here so fast it'll make your head spin." George noticed she was shaking slightly.

"I'm sorry, Doctor Nichols. That's the first time I ever talked like that. I guess I just wasn't thinking. It won't happen again. You can be sure of that."

"No, Schaffer, you had better be sure, because if it does, I'll have you fired. Do you understand?"

"Yes."

"Now, go on and get those patients back to their ward."

While Schaffer was getting his comeuppance, Jubal slipped farther away, down the hallway. Several patients had seen him go, but they said nothing. George was so upset and angry with Dr. Nichols, he never noticed Jubal sneaking off.

Jubal's heart raced. He was determined to get out of the hospital, but he wasn't exactly sure how to do it. However, he knew that to succeed, he had to put more distance between himself and George Schaffer.

When he heard voices coming from up ahead, beyond the turn in the hall, he frantically looked for a place to hide, and as the talking grew louder and closer, he noticed an "Under Construction" sign taped to a nearby restroom door. Quickly he ducked inside and stood motionless. The room was dark and cold, and he waited a good minute or so after the voices passed before switching on the light.

"Lordy ... Lordy," he muttered, seeing the paint cans, drop cloths, ladders, and other tools and equipment that cluttered the L-shaped room. With trembling legs, he crept forward, carefully weaving his way through the mess and rounding the bend in the room, where a draft met him head on.

A paint-splattered tarpaulin hung against a large, multi-paned window, partly concealing it. Gently, Jubal pulled it back from the window.

"Well, I'll be go to heaven!" he chortled. Several panels of the heavy frosted glass were missing, and had been temporarily filled with plywood. Apparently workmen had left things this way for the holiday.

"If this ain't somethin'," Jubal chuckled. "My way out!" With little difficulty, he quietly pulled out one of the wood panels, squeezed through the opening and climbed out. Keeping in the shadows, he made his way off the hospital grounds and went down the long hill into town, where he disappeared in a maze of back streets and alleys, heading towards the southwest.

Cold, damp, and tired, Jubal slipped into the shopping district, and soon arrived in a secluded alley behind a large department store to rest. Minutes later, searching for a way in, he came to a stairwell leading down to a heavy metal door. He tried the handle but it was locked tight.

"Dang it!" he whispered.

But on checking the door closer, he noted the bottom half contained a large section of louvered vents, one corner of which was loose and protruding. "Bingo! This could be the ticket." He pulled and pulled on the vent until little by little it broke free from the door. Setting it aside, he bent down and peered into the darkened basement. Soon Jubal was safely inside.

After making his way upstairs into the large, dimly lit store, and after some searching, Jubal found the department he was looking for. Quickly he went about choosing the things he wanted, stuffing them into a large bag. When he was nearly finished, someone shouted at him. "Hey, what are you doing in here?"

Taken by complete surprise, Jubal swung around to see a uniformed watchman approaching and shining a bright flashlight at him. Jubal picked up his bag, turned and ran as fast as he could. In his wild scramble to get away, he dropped the hand written note he had brought and planned to leave in a conspicuous place for the store people to find.

"Dang!" he said, momentarily stopping, debating whether to go back for it. But with the watchmen coming on, he gave up the idea and resumed his flight.

Jubal made his way back to the basement, and soon to the spot where he had entered the store. Strangely, the watchman was no longer following.

"Some watchman," Jubal chuckled to himself, as he climbed outside with his bag. "The guy didn't seem in too big a hurry to catch me!"

Minutes after Jubal had left, the watchman showed up to discover his exit point, and when he was certain the intruder was indeed gone, he went back to the scene of the crime and made two quick phone calls, one to the police and the other to the store manager, Mr. MacKenzie.

Almost an hour had passed before Jubal's escape was discovered. "Son of a gun!" George Schaffer shouted furiously to another attendant on learning about it. "It's that damned Dr. Nichols. It was all her fault. She got me all off track! Flowers did the very same thing last year on Christmas Eve. We caught him in south Wilberton, but he never said what he was up to."

"Maybe he's going back to finish something," the other man said.

George shrugged. "Maybe ... but maybe he doesn't even have a clue what he's doing. You never know about these clowns."

The police and Dr. Stoddard, the hospital's director, were speedily summoned. They questioned George and other staff members to gather all the facts, wondering if it were possible Flowers could still be in the hospital somewhere.

While the security guards continued searching the building and grounds, George, at the request of the police, retraced his steps towards the dining hall. Checking all the rooms along the way, they discovered the unfinished restroom, and the missing window.

"No doubt about it," George said to the policemen. "He got out right here, through this open window. No doubt about it."

Now that it was confirmed, the information, along with Jubal's description, went out over the police radio, alerting every officer on duty. And, knowing the pattern of his escape the previous year, the search centered in the southwest section of the city.

Around 7:15, in their patrol car and cruising near Slatetown, Tom Watson and Steve Dixon received the radio alert about Jubal's escape with interest. And since the hospital's description of the escapee and the one given by Bernie's night watchman matched, the police quickly deduced that the two incidents were indeed connected.

"Everything's been so quiet out here tonight," Steve said, "I hope we do run into that guy."

"If he shows up in our area," Tom said with confidence, "we'll get him."

CHAPTER XVI

Taking a break from washing the dinner dishes, Stanley went upstairs to check on his mother. Stephanie and the boys were outside on a walking tour of Slatetown, to admire the Christmas lights and decorations. Softly, he crept into her bedroom and found her lying in bed, awake, eyes open and staring blankly at the ceiling.

"Mom," he said in a whisper. "Mom."

Expressionless, she turned her head and looked at him as he came to the side of the bed. "Are you okay?" he asked, stooping to gently brush a ribbon of gray hair from her face.

Making no reply, she kept up her empty stare, until suddenly the corners of her mouth turned upward into a meager but unmistakable smile.

"Mom" he said, buoyed by the change in her expression. "Mom, are you okay? Do you need anything?"

The old woman nodded her head back and forth. "No, I'm all right, Stanley," she said in a weak voice. "I'm fine."

Stanley took her hand and gently squeezed it. "It's so good to hear you talk, Mom," he said.

Her little smile broadened ever so slightly. "What day is this?" she asked.

"Christmas Eve, Mom, the day before Christmas."

Turning pensive, she looked back at the ceiling. Stanley felt as if she might be gazing at some scene from her past, perhaps a bittersweet Christmas memory of old. He kept up his watch until she drifted off to sleep.

"Maybe she's coming around," Stanley said, filled with hope. "God willing!"

Back downstairs, he finished washing the remaining dishes, then picked up the waste can and started for the back door to empty the trash. Suddenly an overwhelming sense of fatigue swept over him, stopping him in his tracks and causing him to set the can back down in place. He decided to take the trash out later.

In the living room, he turned on the TV and collapsed into his easy chair. He was already dozing off when he heard voices and footsteps on the front porch. The door flew open and, along with a blast of cold air, Stephanie came in, wrapped in a heavy coat and red Christmas scarf. Raymond and Edward quickly followed. The excited youngsters ran right to their uncle's side.

"Uncle Stanley," Raymond cried. "You shoulda gone with us!"

"Yeah," Edward chimed in, "you should see the lights and decorations all over Slatetown!"

"We saw the baby Jesus, and Mary and Joseph in front of St. Stanislaus Church," Raymond said. "There was a big, bright star and the Wise Men were there, too. It was all lit up and really neat."

Sleepily, Stanley answered, "Sounds like you had a good time. Any sign of snow?"

"Nah," said Raymond, looking disappointed. "I don't think it's gonna snow tonight."

"Cheer up. There's still time. It may snow yet."

"Okay, boys," Stephanie interjected, "go take off your jackets and hang them in the kitchen. It's almost eight o'clock and time for bed."

"All right, Mom, we're going," said Raymond. "But will Uncle Stanley tell us a story?"

"I don't know," Stephanie said, glancing at her brother. "You'll have to ask him."

Stanley nodded, coming out of his drowsiness. "You guys do what your mother told you and I'll tell you a story."

"Hot dogs!" Raymond exclaimed as he and his brother raced for the kitchen.

After they'd gone, Stephanie tossed her scarf and coat on the sofa. "Try to cheer up, Stan. Things will be better, you'll see."

"I know, I know," he said in a low voice. "I'm trying, really I am." Leaning forward, he added, "I've been praying for a miracle, some good news. I even prayed for snow. It might take the edge off the boys' disappointment tomorrow."

"They'll be fine." Stephanie smiled. "Oh, by the way, I noticed something peculiar while we were out."

"What's that?"

"There were a lot of police cars around, and up by St. Stanislaus, there were two of them parked by the side of the school. I think they were questioning someone."

"Maybe they caught somebody stealing a car or something." Stanley suggested. "Who knows? Did you happen to see Tom and his partner?"

"No," she replied, "I don't think so."

"Maybe they're not working tonight." Stanley got up and turned off the television set.

Just then Raymond and Edward burst back into the living room.

"You guys go up and get washed and ready for bed," Stanley told them. "When you're all set, I'll come up and tell you a story."

"Okay, okay," they shouted as they flew up the stairway.

"Be quiet!" Stephanie called after them. "Don't disturb Mom-mom."

When Stanley came in to the boys' bedroom, they were sitting up with their mother waiting for him. The room was left dark except for the light coming in from the hallway.

Stanley sat down on the edge of the bed. "You guys ready?"

"Yeah. Tell us a Christmas story, Uncle Stanley."

"All right, but let me think for a minute." Looking at the ceiling, he concentrated on composing a tale. In the midst of his contemplations, a loud noise downstairs startled them all.

"What in the world was that?" Stephanie gasped.

"What was it, Uncle Stanley?" added Edward.

"I don't know," said Stanley, getting up. "But I'm gonna find out." He moved cautiously to the door. "Sounded like it came from the kitchen."

Just then there was another noise, followed by a low voice muttering something in an angry tone.

"Oh, my God!" exclaimed Stephanie. "Someone's down there."

Jubal's Christmas Gift

Raymond and Edward disappeared under the covers.

"Stay calm and be quiet," whispered Stanley, as he took the lamp from the dresser and removed its shade. "Stay with the boys, Stephie. I'm going down." He unplugged the cord and wrapped it tightly around the base of the lamp and then, carrying it like a club, he went to the stairs.

"Be careful," Stephanie called to him in a whisper, moving closer to her boys.

CHAPTER XVII

Stanley went down the stairs and cautiously checked the living room. It appeared undisturbed. The tree still twinkled brightly and everything else was in order. He crept on into the darkened dining room. Suddenly, there was a bumping sound coming from the kitchen, confirming his hunch. Holding the lamp high, he padded to the kitchen doorway, flicked on the light, and then quickly stepped inside, ready to clobber anything that moved.

He could hardly believe his eyes! A disheveled old black man, Jubal Flowers, had come in through the back door and was now on all fours, half way under the kitchen table. Every bit as surprising, the man wore a red Santa Claus coat trimmed in white, a matching cap, wide black belt and gloves. His full white beard was his own. But the rest of his outfit, brown trousers and shoes, were glaringly out of place. The waste can that Stanley had left by the door earlier was knocked over on its side. Looking the stranger over, Stanley didn't know what to think. He remained on guard.

"What in the name of heaven is going on here?" he demanded, lowering the lamp and leaning down to get a better look at the elderly man. "If you're a thief, you've come to the wrong house, buddy."

Jubal came out from under the table and sat up on the floor. "Do I look like a thief?" he snapped. "And who leaves a trashcan in the middle of the floor? I darned near broke my neck tripping over it." Jubal shook his head angrily.

Jubal's Christmas Gift

"Serves you right," retorted Stanley, irately. "You break into my home on Christmas Eve, scare the heck out of everybody and then complain about a waste can! That's what I call nerve. I ought to knock your head off." Once again he held the lamp up threateningly.

"Stan, who's down there?" Stephanie called. "Are you all right?"

"Everything's fine," he repeated. "Stay up there and keep the boys with you. Keep them upstairs."

"I didn't break in," Jubal said. "The door was open. I didn't mean to scare anybody, and I sure ain't no thief. I came here for a reason. So quit your jabberin' and give me a hand up."

Stanley thought about calling the police, but instead, he set the lamp on the kitchen counter and took Jubal's hand, helping him to his feet.

"Who are you, anyway?" he asked, taking a closer look at the stranger.

Jubal didn't answer immediately. He was too busy straightening his outfit and brushing off his coat. After Stanley repeated the question, Jubal said. "I'm Santa Claus! Who do think I am?"

"If you're Santa Claus, I'm the Easter bunny."

"Want a carrot?"

"Very funny," Stanley said. "Now one more time, or I'm callin' the cops. Who are you, and what are you doing here in my house?"

"I'm Santa Claus, I tell you."

Suddenly Stanley chuckled.

"What's so funny?" asked Jubal, indignantly.

Stephanie called from the top of the stairs. "Who are you talking to, Stan? What's going on down there?"

"Everything's fine," he assured her. "Stay upstairs, and keep the boys with you. I'll be up in a minute." He turned to Jubal, and said, "Ok, who put you up to this? Was it Tom Watson? I'll bet it was Tom. It must have been."

Jubal shook his head. "Don't know no Tom Watson, and don't care to."

"Come on, it was Tom, wasn't it?"

"No! Nobody sent me."

Stanley thought he had it figured out, but now he wasn't so sure. "If it wasn't Tom, then it must have been one of the guys from work. Yeah, that's it! I'll bet it was Brass. Was it Daryl Brass?"

"Don't know him either," Jubal said. "I told you nobody sent me. I came here on my own, to –"

Stanley interrupted him again, saying, "Okay! Okay! You're Santa Claus and you've just come from the North Pole. But where's the rest of your outfit? And straighten your hat. It looks ridiculous."

Jubal pulled his hat into place and explained, "I didn't have time to get, I mean, Santa was in a big hurry this year." Sticking his jaw out, he asserted, "And I don't like your wisecracks. It wasn't so easy gettin' here, luggin' that bag across town."

"Bag?" Stanley said, looking around the room. "What bag?"

"Santa's bag. I left it outside."

Hearing this, Stanley became more curious and unsure of what was going on. "Okay, okay, I give up," he conceded. "But I'm not in the mood for this or for any more problems. I got enough already."

"Not in the mood for Christmas!" Jubal complained, with a shake of his head. "Nobody but an old Scrooge says that. What's your problem?"

"None of your business," Stanley snapped with an indignant look.

"Ah, so you got problems," Jubal said. "Well, you aren't alone. Everybody's got 'em — but you can't let 'em spoil Christmas."

Stanley shrugged his shoulders and shook his head.

"And by the way, I heard you say you have boys upstairs. How old are they?"

"Six and eight, my sister's kids. She's a widow."

"They your troubles?"

"No!" Stanley said emphatically.

"That's good. Anybody else livin' here?"

"My sister and mother, who's depressed."

"She your trouble?"

"Part of it," Stanley confessed.

"What else?" Jubal asked.

Stanley frowned. "Hey, what is this?" he demanded. "Why should I be telling you, a perfect stranger, my family history?"

"Good God, Gerty!" Jubal cried. "Because I'm Santa Claus. Remember? Now, what else? There's gotta be more."

"I'm losing my job, I'm broke, and my nephews aren't getting *jack* for Christmas. How's that for a Christmas carol?"

Jubal's Christmas Gift

Jubal sighed, and scratched his beard. "Heck, it ain't so good, but I thought you were gonna tell me something really bad."

"It's bad enough!"

Suddenly, Stephanie called down again, "Stan, who are you talking to?"

He started to answer, when Jubal declared, "Hold on a minute, son. I got an idea, a change in plans! Stay right here."

Jubal rushed outside, and returned with a large bag slung over his shoulder.

Stephanie called again. "I'm coming down!"

"No," Stanley shouted, "stay up there! I'll be up in a minute." Turning to Jubal, he said, "Now what in the world are you doing with that?"

Jubal didn't answer. Instead he dropped the bag onto the floor and began searching through it for something. "Where did I put 'em," he said. "I know they're in here.... Ah, found 'em!" He pulled out a string of sleigh bells, and with a sudden, "Outta my way," he slipped past Stanley and rushed out of the kitchen, jingling the bells loudly.

"Hey, come back here," Stanley cried, going after him.

Jubal stopped in the living room, at the foot of the stairway and shouted, "Ho, ho, ho! Merry Christmas, Merry Christmas!"

Angry, Stanley grabbed him by the shoulder. "I knew I should have tossed you out," he said, pulling him away from the stairs. "What do you think you're doing?"

"Hey, let go!" Jubal complained, trying to break free. "You're messin' up my coat."

Stanley pulled him back from the stairs, but the stubborn old man kept jingling his sleigh bells and shouting, "Ho, ho, ho! Merry Christmas! Merry Christmas!"

Raymond and Edward didn't know what to make of the commotion at first, but the merry voice and bells soon proved irresistible. They came out from beneath the covers, and raced fearlessly past their bewildered mother and down the steps. Stephanie followed and, stopping short of the bottom, watched in amazement as her brother struggled with the strangest looking Santa Claus she had ever seen.

"Merry Christmas, Merry Christmas!" Jubal cried.

The joy and excitement expressed in his nephews' eyes were too much for Stanley. Thrusting all caution aside, he let go of the old man.

Jubal straightened his coat and hat, and then pulled the boys close, laughing out loudly, "Merry Christmas, fellas, Merry Christmas!"

"Who are you?" Raymond asked.

"Why I'm Santa Claus," he said. "And I've come to wish you all a very Merry Christmas."

CHAPTER XVIII

Raymond laughed along with Jubal, as the old man insisted he really was Santa. But Edward stared at the stranger and defiantly declared, "You're not Santa Claus!"

Stanley watched closely as Jubal knelt beside Edward and answered, "Oh, no? Why do you say that?"

Edward backed up a step. "'Cause everybody knows Santa Claus isn't black, he's white, 'cause he lives at the North Pole where it snows all the time."

"Well, Good God, Gerty!" Jubal declared, looking surprised and offended. "How do you know that? I'll bet you never seen the real Santa before. And I bet you've never been to the North Pole, either, have ya?"

Edward shook his head.

"Ask your uncle. He'll tell you who I am!" Jubal dared.

Stanley felt the heat of everyone's eyes suddenly on him.

"Is he, Uncle Stanley?" asked the boys. "Is he really Santa Claus?"

For a few eager moments there was a hush in the room as Stanley, staring at Jubal, thought how best to answer. Suddenly, it came to him very clearly, "Sure he's Santa Claus," he declared. "He must be."

On the stairs, Stephanie put a hand to her mouth and smiled.

Ringing his bells, Jubal took the smiling, giggling boys by the hands and led them in an impromptu dance around the room.

Jubal sang: *"Hark! The herald angels sing, glory to the newborn King!"* The boys, Stanley, and Stephanie joined in.

"Peace on earth and mercy mild, God and sinners reconciled. Joyful, all ye nations rise, join the triumph of the skies. With angelic host proclaim, Christ is born in Bethlehem. Hark! The herald angels sing, glory to the newborn King!"

Breathing heavily, Santa finally finished and fell into Stanley's chair to rest. The others all clapped. Soon, though, Raymond and Edward climbed onto his lap and began questioning him about the North Pole, his sleigh, reindeer, and Mrs. Claus. Stephanie, coming down from the stairway with a big smile, took Stanley by the arm. "Who is he?" she quietly asked.

With his eyes fixed on the jolly old man, Stanley declared, "I don't have any idea. Maybe Tom sent him. But he insists he's Santa Claus, and I'm beginning to believe him. Just look at the boys!"

Cocking her head slightly, Stephanie declared, "I don't believe a word of it. You had this planned all along, didn't you?"

"No, honestly, I didn't," he replied, sharply. "I've never seen him before tonight."

"Oh sure," said Stephanie, folding her arms and shaking her head doubtfully.

Jubal suddenly popped up from the chair, bouncing the youngsters to the floor. "Lord have mercy!" he exclaimed, "I almost forgot. Santa's got a surprise for you guys." Briskly, he walked toward the kitchen, but remembering something else, he abruptly stopped and called back to Raymond and Edward. "Have you guys been good all year? Tell me honest!"

"Yes, yes!" they replied, nodding their heads.

"Ain't fibbin' are ya?"

"No, Santa, we wouldn't do that."

"They've been very good," Stephanie said. "And a big help, too."

Jubal's face lit up. "Perfect," he said, "that's just what I wanted to hear. Now everybody stay put and I'll be right back." With that, he disappeared into the kitchen.

While he was gone, the boys did exactly as they were told and stood like statues, with eager smiles that stretched from ear to ear.

"What's he doing?" Stephanie quietly asked her brother.

"Shh," replied Stanley with a forefinger pressed to his lips. "You'll see, you'll see." In the twinkling light of the Christmas tree, he wiped a tear from his eye.

A few moments later, Jubal's voice boomed from the kitchen. "Ho, ho, ho," he called. "Merry Christmas, Merry Christmas." He emerged with a flourish, his bag slung over a shoulder and his sleigh bells dangling and jingling.

Raymond and Edward jumped up and down with excitement, their eyes glowing even brighter than Jubal's.

"Oh, my gosh!" Stephanie cried.

"Excuse me," Santa said politely as he stepped past her and put his bag down by the tree. "Come here, fellas," he told the boys. "I've got some presents for you."

They were at his side almost before he finished the sentence. To their utter delight, the strange Santa Claus pulled a miniature racing car from his sack and gave it to Raymond, who took it with a loud, "Thank you, Santa."

Next, Jubal pulled out a toy dump truck and, with a laugh, gave it to a wide-eyed Edward. "Thank you, Santa," the little boy yelled, then turned to show his mother and Stanley his gift.

Jubal continued pulling gift after gift from his sack for the boys, including a baseball and bat, an AFX Auto Raceway Set, an official NFL football, a Nerf Rocket, a handheld electronic baseball game and a soccer game, a flashlight, Walkie-Talkies, an Erector Set and a couple of funny hats.

"And last but not least," he declared with a laugh, starting to pull out a flat board-like object.

"Skateboards!" the boys shouted with delight.

But when Jubal took out the final gift, he noticed a sudden drop in their enthusiasm. "I'm afraid it's not skateboards, boys," he said. "But you're going to have a lot of fun with this air hockey set. You can play hockey anywhere!"

Raymond and Edward took the box and quietly looked over the enticing illustrations on the cover – and their disappointment vanished. "Wow, this is really cool!" Raymond said. "Air hockey!"

"Yeah," Edward added, "now we can play hockey in our room!"

Excitedly, they hugged Santa and thanked him again and again.

"You're welcome, boys!" Jubal said with a laugh, as the boys started to play with their presents.

"Thank you, Santa," Stanley said. "I don't know what else to say."

"Yes, thank you very much, Santa," Stephanie added, moving closer to the stranger.

Jubal nodded and smiled with satisfaction.

Suddenly Edward spoke up. "Hey, shouldn't we give Santa something?"

"What's that, Edward?" Stanley asked.

"Since he brought us all these really neat toys, shouldn't we give him something, too?"

"No, no!" Jubal protested. "All I want is to see a smile on everyone's face and you've already given me that."

"I got it!" Raymond said. "How about something to eat? Every year we fix Santa a snack and leave it in the kitchen, but this year we forgot."

Flushing with embarrassment, Stephanie said, "Oh, yes! Please forgive me, Santa. With all this excitement, I forgot my manners. But then, we don't have Santa Claus in our home every day."

"I understand," Jubal reassured her. "It's all right."

Stephanie went on, "Please, come out to the kitchen for something to eat."

Jubal cocked his head with interest. "Santa's never been known to turn down any vittles, especially ribs and black-eyed peas, if you got 'em."

Both Stanley and Stephanie laughed. "Well," she responded, "we don't have that, but we do have a nice ham and plenty of potato salad."

"That'll do just fine," said Santa, eagerly glancing towards the kitchen. "Just fine."

From the floor, Edward asked, "Do black-eyed peas come from the North Pole?"

All but the youngsters laughed at the question. Jubal answered, "No, but Santa has 'em flown in special on the reindeer express."

CHAPTER XIX

Leaving the boys with their toys, Stephanie, Stanley and Jubal went into the kitchen. At the table, the two men talked as Stephanie opened the refrigerator and placed the ham, potato salad and condiments in front of them. She set the rye bread on the table and put some rings of the kielbasa onto the stove to cook. Stanley offered Jubal a beer, but he declined, saying it wouldn't look right for the boys to see Santa drinking beer.

When Stephanie sat down with them, she was startled when Stanley introduced himself and her.

"Stan, you mean you really didn't arrange this?" she asked.

"No. I'm just as surprised as you are." He turned to Jubal. "And there's something else I don't understand. If nobody put you up to this, then why did you come here? Why our house? With so many needy black kids around town, why did you pick our house?"

Struggling with a bite of ham sandwich, Jubal did not answer at once. "Well, to tell ya the truth," he soon began, wiping his mouth and beard with a napkin, "I had planned to take them toys to the family mission not so far from here, but, when I met you all, well, I changed my mind. The good Lord don't give a hoot about what color the kids are that gets them toys! And neither do I. Need is need and a good deed is a good deed." He closed with a big grin.

Deeply moved, Stanley and Stephanie sat silent, staring at Jubal, whose attention had moved to the potato salad on his plate.

"But Santa," Stephanie finally said, "you still haven't told us why you picked this house. Why our house? I just don't understand."

No sooner had she asked this question, there was a sudden loud knock at the front door.

"Who can that be?" Stephanie said, looking puzzled

Stanley excused himself and, with Stephanie following, went to answer it. But by the time they reached the door, the boys had already opened it and all were surprised to see their neighbor standing on the porch.

"Mr. Gaska," Stanley greeted him. "Come in, come in!" He showed the man into the warm living room.

"Merry Christmas, folks!" Walter exclaimed.

Wearing a long woolen overcoat with a hood trimmed in fur, he looked like an Eskimo. Besides the distinct odor of coal about him, Stephanie and Stanley both noticed a bulge beneath his coat, just above his waistline. He kept an arm bent and pressed against it. Even stranger, the bulge seemed to be moving.

"Merry Christmas!" they returned to their neighbor.

"Can I take your coat, Mr. Gaska?" Stephanie asked.

"Not just yet," he said. He looked down at the boys. "I was hoping you two would still be up and not already in bed."

"We were in bed..." said Raymond.

"But," Edward interrupted, "Santa Claus came and brought us all these presents."

Mr. Gaska laughed. "It sure looks like he was here, all right," he said, surprised to see the many gifts.

"He's still here!" Edward declared. "He's in the kitchen."

Gaska's smile gave way to a puzzled look.

"That's right, Mr. Gaska," Stanley corroborated. "Santa's in the kitchen eating."

Stephanie intervened. "Would you like to come back and meet him? You're welcome to have something to eat, too."

"I'd like that very much, but first I have a little something for the boys for Christmas. I'm afraid it doesn't compare to all this here, but I wanted to do something nice for them, especially this year."

He carefully unbuttoned his coat and, to everyone's surprise, Zigzag's familiar face popped out and let out a loud meow.

"Zigzag!" shouted the boys. Taking him into their arms, they hugged him close.

"Where did you find him?" asked Raymond, nose-to-nose with Zigzag.

"On my front porch, late this afternoon, he was sittin' there by the door, just like he had never been gone."

"Wow!" exclaimed Edward, "I thought he'd never come home."

"This time," said Gaska, "I almost did too." Turning to Stanley and Stephanie, he said, "If it's okay with your mother and your uncle, you can have Zigzag." Then, looking back at the boys, he added, "He likes you two a lot better than me. I'm too old to play with him."

"Thanks, Mr. Gaska," they replied, hugging the cat closer. "Can we keep him, Mom? Can we?"

Stephanie looked at her brother. "It's all right with me," she said.

"Then it's all right with me, too."

"Yay, yay!" the boys shouted, jumping up and down. "Thank you, Mr. Gaska!"

"All right, boys," Stephanie said. "We're going to the kitchen to see Santa Claus and get Mr. Gaska something to eat."

"Okay, Mom," Raymond responded. "We'll play with Zigzag and our toys."

In the kitchen, Walter Gaska was introduced to Santa Claus. He didn't ask about the stranger's real identity, feeling certain his neighbors surely knew the man and had put him up to the charade for the boys' sake. Walter just laughed and went along with it.

So there, at the kitchen table, they all sat eating, drinking, laughing, and having a great old time. Sidetracked by the interruptions and so caught up in the moment, Stanley and Stephanie didn't resume questioning Jubal about who he was, where he had come from, or why he had picked their home. Although they let the questions go for the time being, they were determined to get the answers before Jubal left their home. Yet, by now, Jubal had dispelled all of Stanley and Stephanie's lingering fears and suspicions. They felt certain there was something very special about the old man.

81

CHAPTER XX

Shortly after Walter Gaska arrived, there was another loud knock at the front door. Stanley jumped up from the table, wondering aloud, "Now what? This is becoming quite a night." He hurried past the boys, who were busy playing with Zigzag and their toys, to see who was at the door.

Outside, a police car's flashing emergency lights bathed the street in a reddish glow. Tom Watson stood on the porch, while Steve Dixon sat at the wheel.

"Hey, Tom!" Stanley exclaimed, smiling broadly. "Merry Christmas, buddy. I'm really glad you stopped by."

"Merry Christmas, Stan," Tom replied. "You look in high spirits."

"Come on in. We're out in the kitchen. There's plenty to eat and drink. Tell Steve to come in, too."

"I'd love to, but we can't. We've got something going on."

"All right, but you're missing quite a party. We haven't had so much fun around here in years. You won't believe it. Guess who …"

Tom interrupted him. "Sorry to cut you off, Stan, but we're looking for a guy, and he was spotted here in Slatetown. You haven't seen a short black man in a Santa Claus outfit, have you?"

Stanley's mouth fell open, and his good spirits nosedived.

Noticing his sudden change of mood, Tom asked again, "You've seen him?"

Jubal's Christmas Gift

Stepping out onto the porch, Stanley pulled the door half closed behind him and, facing the officer again, said, "Yeah, I've seen him. Why, what's he done?"

"For starters, he escaped from Ludlow this evening and..."

"The mental hospital?"

"Yep, the hospital. Then he broke into Bernie's Department store. A security guard scared him off, but not before he made off with a Santa Claus outfit and some other stuff. I hear Mr. Kirkpatrick, the owner, was stormin' mad when he got the word. He and his store manager are out here looking for the guy, too. Flaherty has them in his car. Now, where'd you see him?"

Stanley's mind whirled, digesting the startling information. "Is he dangerous?"

"No," Tom replied. "At least the hospital says he's not. He's scheduled for discharge sometime in January. He's been a long termer. He got admitted years ago after some kind of a mental breakdown, and has been in and out ever since. They say he's better now, but since he doesn't have any family or friends that they know of, they can't figure out why he took off. Now, come on, Stan, I'm in a hurry. We have cops all over Slatetown looking for the guy. Where did you see him?"

Shivering in the cold, Stanley stared blankly, deep in thought, realizing he had to come out with it. "He's here in the house."

Tom took a half step forward. "You're kidding!" he exclaimed, eagerly looking around Stanley, trying to see into the house.

"No, I'm not. He's here all right. He's been here for a while, and just like you said, he's dressed like Santa Claus."

"Well, what do you know! He's right here, in your house."

After a pause, Tom assumed an official tone: "Ok, you keep him in there while I go tell Steve to call it in. We'll get a hospital ambulance out here on the double. I don't think we'll have any trouble with the old guy, but we might have some keeping Kirkpatrick calm. Like I said, I hear he's pretty mad. He couldn't believe anyone would rob his store on Christmas Eve. Maybe he'll feel better when he finds out he's getting his stolen merchandise back."

As Tom started to leave the porch, Stanley grabbed his arm. "Wait a minute, Tom," he urged. "I think that old man might really be Santa Claus. And I'm not going to let you storm in here and take him, not in front of the boys. No way!"

Tom almost fell off the porch. "What?" he cried. "What's the matter with you? You sound like you're ready for Ludlow Hospital, too."

"Maybe I am, but if that guy isn't Santa Clause, he's the next best thing. We all think so, even Mr. Gaska, our neighbor. Raymond and Edward are positively certain he's Santa Claus."

Tom laughed. "Okay, okay, calm down. I can see I'm missing something here. Why don't you just start from the beginning and let me have it all. What's going on?"

Stanley took a deep breath and began: "He came in through our kitchen about an hour ago. Why our house, I have no idea, and he hasn't said, but he scared the heck out of us all. I found him on the kitchen floor. He had tripped over our trashcan. At first, I almost crowned him with a lamp, but there was something about him that stopped me. I can't explain it."

Stanley paused, then broke into a chuckle and went on, "He's sure not from the North Pole, but he's a likable, funny old guy. You should have seen him laughing with the boys, dancing, and singing. I thought maybe you sent him, Tom."

"Me?" Tom laughed with surprise.

"Yeah, I just couldn't figure it, why he came to our house. Anyway, Raymond and Edward just love him and he's brought a lot of cheer into a sad house. Sure there was something fishy about it all, but I didn't care. It was like a miracle. For the first time in months, I was laughing and enjoying myself."

"But he's got to go back," Tom said.

"Heck, I know that, but what am I going to tell the boys? And what's going to happen to all the presents he gave them?"

"Presents?" said Tom, his eyebrows arching upwards.

"Yeah, presents! He must have taken those toys from Bernie's and lugged them all the way here. God only knows why he came here, but he couldn't have picked a better house."

"He gave them to the boys?" laughed Tom.

"Yeah, pulled them out of a bag just like Santa Claus. It'll break their hearts to have to give them up now. Since things have gotten so tight, I could barely afford one lousy present apiece for them, and they weren't much. Now, do you see why I say this jolly old black man might be Santa Claus?"

The officer laughed and shook his head. "This is too much, Stan, just incredible."

"You're telling me."

Turning official again, Tom said, "All right, all right, I'll figure out something. Now, let's go out to the car, I gotta have Steve radio this in right away. I'll see what I can do with Kirkpatrick, too."

"Thanks, Tom, thanks so much."

All the way to the car, Tom chuckled to himself. After telling Steve of the development, he ordered him to call Officer Flaherty and have him bring Kirkpatrick and MacKenzie to their location. Tom also instructed Steve to call headquarters and let them know the patient has been found and to request that Ludlow Hospital send an ambulance to 408 Hickory Street in Slatetown.

Within minutes, Officer Flaherty, who was nearby on the hunt too, drove his squad car onto the street and parked nearby. Mr. Kirkpatrick and Mac MacKenzie quickly got out and made their way to Sergeant Watson. Kirkpatrick wasted no time introducing himself and his store manager.

"I understand you've found the man," Kirkpatrick said to the sergeant in a gruff, angry voice.

"Yes, Mr. Kirkpatrick," said Tom, "he's here in this house."

"Well, go in and arrest him! He had the gall to rob my store on Christmas Eve. What kind of a man would do that? I want you to throw the book at the guy."

Stanley suddenly interrupted, "No, no, you don't understand, Mr. Kirkpatrick! "

"Who is this?" Kirkpatrick angrily asked the officer.

"Stanley Wisniewski, sir, an old friend of mine," Tom replied. "He owns this house."

"Nice to meet you, Mr. Kirkpatrick," said Stanley. He extended his hand, but the elder man ignored it.

Turning to Tom, Kirkpatrick said, "I don't care to meet your friend or anyone else right now, Sergeant. I just want you to arrest that guy and return my stolen property. Is that clear?"

At that, Stanley shouted, "Now listen here, you." But Tom quickly stopped him.

"Hold it, Stan!" he ordered. "Mr. Kirkpatrick may be a bit harsh, but he's perfectly within his rights. Now, I want you to get into my car with Officer Dixon and keep quiet, do you understand?" When Stanley grudgingly nodded, he added, "Get in there and cool off — or warm up, I should say. You're going to catch pneumonia out here without a coat. I'll call you out when I'm ready."

Dennis D. Skirvin

"But—" Stanley started to protest.

"Get in the car or I'll arrest you for obstructing justice. I want to explain a few things to Mr. Kirkpatrick and his associate in private."

Reluctantly, Stanley did as he was ordered. And once inside the patrol car, he related the whole story to Steve, who couldn't help laughing, too. Afterward, Steve relayed the details to the other officers who had converged on the street. The whole block was bathed in red flashing lights coming from the police cars.

Finally, Tom asked Stanley to get out of the car. He was still talking with Kirkpatrick and MacKenzie and two plainclothes detectives when Stanley stepped back out into the street. Right away he noted that Mr. Kirkpatrick seemed to have mellowed.

"We'd like to question you about all of this, Mr. Wisniewski," one of the detectives told Stanley, "but we're going to hold off for now."

Stanley nodded. "Sure, that's fine."

Then Tom told Stanley, "Your family knows Steve and me, so we're going back in with you. I promise we'll be discreet."

Mr. Kirkpatrick quickly spoke up, "And if you don't mind, Mr. Wisniewski, Mr. MacKenzie and I would like to go in too, and meet 'Santa Claus'."

He hardly got the words out when Mac added, "Yes, I hope you're agreeable."

"Sure," Stanley said. "That's fine."

"Thank you, sir," Kirkpatrick said. "And, incidentally, I'd like to apologize to you for my previous rude behavior." He put his hand out to Stanley and the two shook.

"It's okay," Stanley said. "I understand. This hasn't exactly been a normal night for me either." Suddenly, Stanley thought of something. "Oh," he said, "there's just one more thing! While you're in my home, I have to ask you not to bring up the incident at your store. I'd rather you wait until you're all back outside, away from the kids."

"Most certainly!" Mr. Kirkpatrick said, nodding his head. "We understand."

"You have our word on it," Mac added.

"Good," said Stanley. "Thank you."

"If anyone should ask about who we are," Mr. Kirkpatrick said, "maybe you could just say that we're a couple of detectives?"

"No, I'm afraid you can't say that," Tom objected. "We'll just say that you are a couple of businessmen who happened to be with us on another matter when we heard that Santa Claus was here in Stanley's house. We didn't think Stanley would mind if we brought you along to meet Santa, too."

"Perfect!" Stanley said. "That'll work."

"Ok, it's a plan," Tom said. "Hey, Steve, come on. We're going inside."

Quickly, as his young partner joined him, Tom said, "All right now, let's go see Mr. Flowers."

"Who?" Stanley asked.

"Jubal Flowers, that's the guy's name."

"Flowers," Mac repeated the name.

"What's that?" Tom asked him.

"Nothing," Mac replied, thoughtfully. "Just thinking out loud."

"I don't care what his real name is!" Stanley said. "Tonight he's Santa Claus, from the North Pole! Got it?"

"Yeah, sure, Stan," the sergeant replied. "Now let's go see Mr. Claus."

As the men started toward the home, Mac MacKenzie stayed behind, absorbed in deep thought. Noticing him, Mr. Kirkpatrick turned back and asked, "Mac, are you coming? Is there something wrong?"

"No. I don't think so," Mac said, sounding strangely distant.

"Well then, come on!" Kirkpatrick said. "Let's go." But Mac still didn't move, prompting Kirkpatrick to take him by the arm, and ask, "Are you all right?"

"Yes, but there's a chance I might know this guy," Mac confessed.

Surprised, Kirkpatrick said, "Well, if you know him, you know him. You can explain later. Now come on!"

The two quickly caught up to the others as they were about to go into Stanley's home.

CHAPTER XXI

When Stanley led the others into his home, they found Jubal, Stephanie, Mr. Gaska, and the boys all in the living room singing "Silent Night." Jubal in his Santa Claus finery sat in Stanley's easy chair. Raymond and Edward sat on the floor by his feet with Zigzag, and Stephanie and Mr. Gaska stood near the Christmas tree. In all of Slatetown, or the world over for that matter, it's unlikely that one could have found a home or group of people more imbued with the holy spirit of Christmas.

Jubal waved a hello at the policemen, who had joined the singing, along with Mr. Kirkpatrick and Mac MacKenzie. Jubal was almost ready to go with them, but there was still something he had to do. After the song, he led them in a lively rendition of "Jingle Bells."

Finally, when the caroling was finished, they all clapped and cheered. Stephanie welcomed the newcomers into her home. After Stanley made all the introductions according to the plan, Tom Watson, Mr. Kirkpatrick and Mac MacKenzie talked to Jubal, addressing him as Santa Claus since the boys were near.

Kirkpatrick leaned close to Mac, and whispered in his ear, "Do you recognize him?"

"No," Mac said in a low voice, shaking his head. "Not at all."

Jubal noticed that Steve Dixon could barely take his eyes off of Stephanie. *Little wonder,* he thought. In the twinkling light of the Christmas tree, she looked beautiful.

Jubal's Christmas Gift

Steve moved close to her. "Merry Christmas, Stephie," he said. "It's nice to see you and your boys again."

"Merry Christmas, Steve," she replied with a smile. "It's nice to see you, too. But what brings you here tonight?"

The policeman momentarily glanced at Jubal. "It's a strange story. I think you'd really like to hear it. Maybe we could go somewhere a little quieter."

Stephanie looked confused. "Come on, we'll go into the kitchen."

She led the way, but at the doorway, he suddenly caught her by the arm and stopped. "Hold on a second," he said, grinning and pointing upward. "That's mistletoe! It would be bad luck to break with Christmas tradition." Surprising her, he leaned forward and kissed her softly on the cheek.

"Oh sure, tradition," she said, her face flushed with embarrassment. "I understand. I sure wouldn't want to see any bad luck come our way."

As they went on in to the kitchen, Dixon chuckled, "I'm glad to hear that. Now wait 'til you hear what I have to tell you about Santa Claus."

Back by the Christmas tree, Stanley watched as Tom, Mr. Kirkpatrick and Mac MacKenzie talked with Jubal and the boys. Tom questioned Jubal about the North Pole and his reindeer, and the men chuckled at each of his clever replies. They carried out the charade perfectly and always addressed him as Santa. Jubal was quite an impressive and very convincing Santa Claus.

Finally, Tom Watson leaned close to Jubal and said softly, "It's time to go, Mr. Flowers."

Jubal smiled. "Okay, I'm almost ready. There's just one more thing I have to do. Let's go to the kitchen, Stanley. This won't take long."

Stanley looked at Tom, and the policeman quickly nodded his approval. "One more thing?" Stanley said to Jubal. "I don't understand."

"You will," Jubal chuckled. "I have something to give you."

"Something for me?" Stanley asked, confused.

Getting up from his chair, Jubal told the boys, "You guys stay here. Your uncle and I will be right back and then Santa will have to be leaving."

"Aw, do you gotta go?" Raymond whined.

Edward pleaded, "Yeah, can't you stay here tonight with us?"

"I'd love to, boys," Jubal said, "but this is Christmas Eve, and there are still plenty of children waiting for me."

While the boys grumbled with disappointment, Tom Watson took Jubal by the coattail and said, "I'll go along, too, if you don't mind, Santa."

"Sure," Jubal agreed, with a smile. "And all of you gentlemen can come with us, too." To the boys, he said, "Be back in a couple minutes."

"Okay, Santa," Raymond said as the boys went back to playing with Zigzag.

Steve and Stephanie were sitting at the table talking when Jubal and the others came into the kitchen.

"Listen, Santa, you've already given me more than enough," Stanley said. "I don't want anything else."

"Hush," replied Jubal. "You don't have a choice, and it's not really for you anyway."

The others exchanged puzzled looks.

"Now I'm really confused," said Stanley. "I don't understand what you're saying."

"You will," assured Jubal. "But first — I'm sure you all know who I am by now and that I come from Ludlow Hospital?"

Everyone but Mr. Gaska nodded. The antique dealer's brief, "Well, I'll be," gave evidence to his complete surprise.

Jubal sat at the table and explained. "I've had my share of troubles too, Stanley. Lord knows I have. They started long ago and got worse through the years. But once during them dark times, a stranger did something so kind for me that I never forgot it. For years I've thought about what that man did for me, and the debt of kindness I owed him. I wanted to do something good in return. But things got in the way, and I kept puttin' it off until tonight. And now I'm ready to pay it back, or pay it forward as they say."

"Yes," Stanley said, "but I don't understand why you came here, to our house? And why on Christmas Eve?"

Jubal laughed. "The answer to them questions goes back many years, to the time when I was just a young man. I came to Wilberton looking for work. I came from down South with my wife Maggie and my boy. Oh, I loved 'em both, 'bout as much as any man could. We lived in a little, bitty old wooden shack and I could barely keep it up 'cause I couldn't find no job. Good Lord, times was hard back then.

Jubal's Christmas Gift

"One cold, snowy Christmas Eve, can't even remember the year now, I went to see the richest man in Wilberton about a job. He lived in a huge mansion on a hilltop overlookin' town. It's the hospital now. Everyone said I was wastin' my time, that I was crazy. Even Maggie said so. But I heard this man was different, that he was kind and good. So I took my chances and went. And guess what?"

"What, what happened?" Stephanie asked.

Jubal laughed. "Good God, Gerty! He took a likin' to me! He gave me a job, and a place for my family and me to live! It was a sturdy brick house with a gray slate roof and we lived there for nearly two years."

"Where was it, Mr. Flowers?" Steve asked.

"Right here in Slatetown at 408 Hickory Street!"

"Here!" cried Stanley. "You mean you lived here, in this house?"

"That's right, Stanley. We were the only black folk here, but we had no trouble. Some of our Polish neighbors were far worse off than we was. Heck, at least, we could speak English."

Suddenly, Walter Gaska said, "Yes, I remember. A black family did live here then, right before I moved in. At that time, they were still building houses for the immigrants coming from Europe."

"Sure enough," said Jubal. "We were one of the first families to live in this part of Slatetown. The rich man I worked for had these homes built, and he insisted on slate roofs so they'd last a long time. He let us live here for almost nothin'. I'll never forget him, or what he did. He had the biggest heart and was the most generous man I ever know'd. The man's name was Ludlow, Horace T. Ludlow. He was the wealthiest man in Wilberton and he died some years ago."

"Ludlow!" Stanley said in surprise. "He's the guy who owned the plant where I work, the guy with the plaque in City Hall! I can hardly believe it."

"He's the man, all right," Jubal said, getting up slowly from his chair. "I'll never forget him. Now Stanley, I'll need a knife."

Tom Watson, looking concerned, said, "Ah, Mr. Flowers."

Smiling, Jubal assured the sergeant, "Don't worry, Officer, I ain't gonna cut no one."

Everyone looked on as Stanley took a table knife from a drawer and handed it to Jubal.

"This'll work fine," said Jubal. "Now let's get this table away from the wall."

Steve and Jubal moved the table. Jubal got in behind it, next to the wall, and kneeling, he wedged the knife behind a foot-long section of the baseboard molding and began prying it loose. As he worked, he told them, "My wife had a lot of faults, and a rovin' eye was just one of 'em. 'Course the good Lord knows I wasn't no saint either. Not by a long shot. One day I came home from work and found a note sayin' she'd left with some other man. Took my boy, too, my little Billy Boy. Oh, Lordy how I loved that boy. It broke my heart, and I ain't been right ever since that day."

His voice trailed off as the baseboard started to give.

"Ah, it's comin' loose!" he cried as the section popped free from the wall. Everyone leaned in closer for a better view.

Chapter XXII

Beaming with delight, Jubal set the section of baseboard aside and cried, "Just as I'd hoped, it's still in here!" He pulled a small cloth bag from the secret compartment and emptied the contents onto the table — a small, tightly wound roll of bills and some loose change.

"Oh my gosh!" Stephanie gasped.

"Well, I'll be," Mr. Gaska muttered.

With great interest, Kirkpatrick and Mac crowded in to see the money. They listened most attentively as Jubal went on.

"I kept my savings here 'cause I never much trusted in banks," Jubal said. "It's only a hundred dollars or so, but it's all I got. I planned to sneak in here and get my money and use it to pay back the store I took the Santa Claus outfit and toys from. Heck, I didn't think about the outfit until I saw it there tonight. And I woulda got the rest of it 'cept for that guard who scared me off."

The old man paused momentarily, then continued, "I had a note all written out saying I planned to pay for the things I took, but I dropped it when that guard chased me."

On hearing this, Mac quietly reached into his pocket for the paper he had picked up in the aisle before leaving the store for Slatetown.

Jubal continued. "After I met you and your family, Stanley, I changed my mind about goin' to the mission. I didn't have to. There was enough need right here."

The others were speechless, doubting they would ever again see anything as genuinely unselfish as Jubal's Christmas gift. Stanley sat down at the table and stared blankly at the old man. Stephanie threw her arms around him and gave him a kiss on the cheek. "Thank you, Santa," she said, "you're a wonderful, wonderful man." Jubal laughed with delight.

"But why?" Stanley spoke up. "I still don't understand why you did all of this?"

Putting the money back into the bag, Jubal explained, "That's simple. I've been itchin' to do a good deed for someone in need, like Mr. Ludlow did for me, and it had to be at Christmas! That's all. Ludlow said that God had blessed him with wealth, and that doing good for others was a way of givin' Him thanks and praise. He said that doin' good for someone can often move others to do good too, and on and on. He called them God's *goodwill dividends*. I didn't quite get it then, but I came to understand as I got older. I owed him a lot, a real debt of kindness that I just had to repay. He believed in doing good for others, and so do I, and Jubal Flowers ain't no fool."

After a brief silence, Stanley said, "I just don't know what to say, Mr. Flowers. But thank you for what you've done here tonight. You've taught me quite a lesson. Thank you so much."

"You're welcome, Stanley."

"You've taught us all a lesson, Mr. Flowers," Mr. Kirkpatrick added.

"Yes, he has," Mac said.

Jubal smiled and nodded. He held up the small bag, saying, "I'm gonna leave this money with you, Stanley, and ask you to pay that store for them Christmas presents I gave to Raymond and Edward. Will you do that for me?"

Stanley waved a hand in protest. "There's no need for that, Mr. Flowers," he said.

Surprised, Jubal, "What do you mean? I have to pay for those things."

"We weren't going to tell you until you were outside, but I think it's okay to tell you now. The boys aren't here." He looked at Tom, who gave him a nod. Then pointing to Mr. Kirkpatrick, Stanley went on, "This gentleman here, Mr. Flowers, is Mr. Michael Kirkpatrick, the owner of Bernie's, the department store where you got the presents and the outfit."

Surprised, Jubal looked up at the storeowner. "Well Good God, Gerty, what do ya know about that!"

Jubal's Christmas Gift

"And this other gentleman is the store manager, Mac MacKenzie," Stanley said. "You can give them the money right now."

"I'm sorry for any problems I may have caused, Mr. Kirkpatrick, sir," Jubal said sincerely. "Please take this money and if I owe anything more, I'll pay that too, somehow." He held out the bag for Mr. Kirkpatrick.

Kirkpatrick started to protest, but Mac quickly stepped forward and cut him off.

"If I could, I have some things I need to say," the manager said, respectfully. He turned back to Jubal, and went on, "As Mr. Wisniewski said, I'm the manager of the store. Tonight shortly after getting home, I received a phone call from our security people, letting me know of the incident. I wasted no time getting back to the store. The police had just arrived and shortly after, Mr. Kirkpatrick came in. Officer Flaherty, whom we met there, offered to bring us here to Slatetown. On our way out of the store, I noticed a crumpled piece of paper on the floor, your note, but thinking it was trash, I just put it in my pocket."

Jubal lit up with joy. "See! I told you all I left a note!"

Mac held up the crinkled paper. "When you mentioned you had dropped it in the store moments ago, I pulled it from my pocket and quickly read it. If it's okay with you, I'd like to share it with everyone."

Jubal nodded approvingly. "Sure, go ahead."

Mac slowly began to read Jubal's note. "It begins with three capital letters at the very top: I, O, and U. Below them, the same three letters are written again, one on top of the other, and next to the first, the letter I, is the name, *Jubal*. Next to the letter O is the word *owe*, o-w-e, and next to the U are the words, *God Almighty, Mr. Ludlow, and this store*. Below that, you wrote…" But a sudden catch in his voice caused him to pause. The others couldn't help noticing that he was becoming emotional.

Mac drew in a deep breath, and started again, reading: "First, *I owe the good Lord for my life and for giving me the greatest joy I ever knew, my little boy, my little Billy, wherever he might be. Second, I owe Mr. Ludlow, for the lesson he taught me, and the many kindnesses he showed me. And, finally, I owe this store for the things I took to give as Christmas presents to some needy kids in town. I promise to pay for them when I get out of the hospital, which is gonna be soon, Jubal Flowers."*

Quiet engulfed the room as Mac quietly folded the note.

Tom Watson said, "We're going to need that note, if you don't mind, Mr. MacKenzie."

"Oh sure, Sergeant," Mac said, quickly handing it over to the policeman. "But I'd like to get it back at some point, if possible."

"I think we can arrange that," Tom said.

"Now," Mr. Kirkpatrick spoke up, "I'd like to say a few words if I could." But once again Mac quickly cut him off.

"Sorry, sir, but please let me finish. There's more. There's something else I have to say."

Puzzled, Kirkpatrick nevertheless quickly agreed. "Sure, Mac, go right ahead," he said.

A cloud of mystery filled the kitchen as everyone, including Jubal, wondered what in the world Mac MacKenzie could add.

Remaining at the old man's side, Mac pulled his wallet from his back pocket. "I have something that I want everyone to see, especially Mr. Flowers." Searching the wallet and growing more and more emotional, he added, "It's something I've had with me for a long, long time. It's an old photograph of me as a small boy standing between my mother and father." He produced the time-worn, black and white photo, and with tear-filled eyes, fell silent, cherishing the memories it evoked.

"What in the world is going on here?" Mr. Kirkpatrick asked, looking at his friend and employee. "Are you okay, Mac?" he asked.

Mac raised a hand and nodded. "Yes!" he whispered. "There are some words scribbled on the margins of the photo: *Wilberton, NJ* and the names *Maggie, Jubal* and *Billy*, that's me William MacKenzie!"

Everyone gasped in shocked surprise! Jubal jumped out of his chair and took the photograph. "I remember this picture!" he declared, looking at it closely. Then, sobbing, he wrapped his arms around Mac and hugged him close. "Billy!" he cried. "Oh, my God, my boy, my little Billy boy! Is it really you?"

"Yes, it's me!" Mac said, tearfully. "Billy, your son!"

"Lordy, Lordy, Lordy!" Jubal shouted. He kissed him on the cheek, again and again, and held him tight. Looking upward, he went on, "Thank you, Lord! Thank you for this Christmas gift.

Only you know how I've prayed for this day." Overwhelmed, he sat down, lowered his head on to the table, and sobbed.

Profoundly moved by the unexpected reunion, Stephanie wept, too. Stanley, Mr. Gaska, and Mr. Kirkpatrick stood in stunned silence, watching the drama unfold. Steve Dixon put an arm around Stephanie.

Finally, Mr. Kirkpatrick said, "Well, I'll be." Smiling, he shook his head in wonder.

Mr. Gaska wiped tears from his eyes. Tom Watson and Stanley each placed a hand on Jubal's shoulder, before he got up and hugged his son again, rocking him back and forth. "Billy ... Billy ... my Billy boy!" he repeated.

Jubal held up the photograph again, declaring, "I remember this picture. It was taken right here in Slatetown. We were at the park on a Sunday afternoon."

He looked closely at the photo. "Oh, Maggie ... Maggie Butler, look at you! Lordy! And look at me, with dark hair and no white beard. How young we were."

"When my mother took me away," Mac explained, "we moved around a lot, but finally settled outside of Pittsburgh. And as my father said, she wasn't the best mother, but she was *my* mother, and I loved her." He hesitated for a moment before going on.

"I had lots of problems growing up, too many to mention. Life was tough. My mother was mostly absent, but she did one thing I'm forever thankful for. Somehow, she managed to get me into a high school run by Christian friars. A lot of my tuition was paid through charity, but I had to work after school and summers to help pay the rest. That school was hard, but it changed my life."

"Another good deed!" Jubal declared, listening intently to each word, feeling so proud of the man his son had become.

"Since my parents were never married," Mac went on, "my mother gave me her surname of Butler. I didn't know a whole lot about my father, mostly just his name and what little my mother had told me. But I did remember he was always kind to me and to others."

Mr. Kirkpatrick suddenly said, "I'm a little confused, Mac. How did you go from Butler to MacKenzie?"

Before Mac could answer, Jubal spoke up. "I think I can explain it," he said. "Check me if I'm wrong," he went on, looking at his son. "When your mother ran off, taking you with her, she went with a man by the name of Frank MacKenzie. That right?"

"That's right," Mac said. "He became my step-father."

"I knew it!" Jubal said, "I knew it. I had a suspicion all along that's what happened, but now I know for sure."

"My mother married him when I was still a boy, and she insisted he adopt me. That's how I became William MacKenzie. Growing up, everyone called me Mac, so I became Mac MacKenzie!"

"Well I'll be go to heaven!" Jubal declared.

"Then that explains it," Mr. Kirkpatrick said. "Mystery solved."

Mac went on with his explanation. "I went to college and got my business degree and worked around the Pittsburgh area at various jobs for a few years, until finally landing a job at Mr. Kirkpatrick's Pittsburgh store. My step-father died six years ago, and when my mother died four years later, I decided I needed to know more about my father. By chance, an opportunity arose to transfer to the Wilberton store, and I jumped on it."

"So glad you did, Mac," Mr. Kirkpatrick cheerfully interjected.

"Me too!" said Jubal.

"Soon after moving here, I started looking for you, Dad, but had no luck. I never thought to look in the Ludlow Hospital." Mac fell quiet for a few moments, thinking. "It's so strange," he began again, sounding a bit philosophical, "how all of this has worked out, especially on Christmas Eve of all times."

"God works in mysterious ways!" Walter Gaska observed.

"He sure does," Jubal quickly agreed. "And surely His hand is in this."

"Amen to that," Mr. Kirkpatrick said, and the others all agreed.

Just then, Raymond, wild-eyed with excitement, suddenly burst into the kitchen, shouting, "Uncle Stanley, the police are at the door! They came for Santa Claus."

With this news, the joyous mood in the kitchen suddenly turned solemn.

After thanking Raymond, Tom turned to Jubal. "I hate to be the one to say this, Santa," he said, "but it's time to go."

But even this inevitability didn't lower Jubal's spirits. "I understand, Officer," he said. "No problem." And turning to his son, he declared: "I don't care what others might call you, but you'll always be Billy to me. My little Billy boy. Merry Christmas, son. I love you!"

Jubal's Christmas Gift

"Merry Christmas, Dad," Mac replied. "I love you, too."

Jubal shouted to the others, "Merry Christmas to everyone!" And with great joy, the others all returned the wish.

Raymond took one of the old man's hands, shouting, "I can show Santa to the door."

Mac took Jubal's other hand, as the excited youngster led Santa out of the kitchen. Stephanie, Steve, Walter and Tom followed. Mr. Kirkpatrick lingered behind, buttonholing Stanley in the doorway.

"I've never seen anything like this in all my life!" the storeowner said ecstatically. "If I wasn't here to witness it, I don't know if I would have believed it. And to think he comes from Ludlow Hospital! It just doesn't seem possible. We need more people like him in this world."

Stanley nodded in full agreement. "We sure do!"

Drawing closer to Stanley and speaking in a low voice, Kirkpatrick went on. "You know, Wisniewski, Christmas comes and goes every year and, just like so many people, I often take it for granted, but this year I've been touched, really touched. What happened tonight has just made that feeling more meaningful. So, without saying more, I'd like you to consider all these toys that Mr. Flowers, that is, Santa, brought as a gift from my department store." He stopped and pointed to the small bag on the table. "As for the money, hold on to it, and make sure Santa gets it back. Oh, and please don't tell the boys, at least not until they're older." On this last point, he was quite emphatic.

"Thank you, Mr. Kirkpatrick, thank you," said Stanley, shaking the man's hand. "That's a big relief, and very kind of you. I'll never forget it."

Kirkpatrick laughed. "There's one more thing. I understand you'll be out of work in a couple of days."

"That's right. I work at LudMore Rubber and I'm sure you've read about what's going on there."

"Oh yes I have, and it's a real shame." Kirkpatrick glanced towards the living room and hurriedly continued. "We can talk more about this later, but we're in the process of enlarging our hardware department at the store, and we need good people, mechanically inclined people, to staff it. If you're interested in a steady job with good benefits, give me a call."

"Interested?" Stanley cried, nearly overwhelmed. "Sure I'm interested! I don't know what to say. Thank you, Mr. Kirkpatrick. Thank you so much."

"You're welcome. Oh and one final thing!" Kirkpatrick said. "Real quick before Santa leaves. Ironically enough, I'm part of a group that's protesting the removal of some very meaningful words from city hall, a quotation about doing good for others."

"The Ludlow plaque!" Stanley said, remembering. "I knew you looked familiar. I saw you on TV."

"That's right. And with your help, that plaque will go back on display. What happened here tonight must be told, and believe me, the mayor's going to hear about it. The world might be growing colder, Wisniewski, but there are still plenty of good people in it. Now, let's hurry before Santa Claus leaves."

CHAPTER XXIII

M r. Kirkpatrick rushed out of the kitchen to join the others, but Stanley held back in the doorway, wiping tears from his eyes, and offering a quick prayer, thanking God for all that had happened. Then, feeling happier than he had in months, he went into the living room and joined the others.

Jubal, holding Raymond and Edward in his arms, stood by the door next to Mac.

"Can't we go outside with you, Santa?" Raymond pleaded.

"Yeah," his little brother chimed in, "we want to see your sleigh and reindeer."

Jubal laughed. "Maybe next year, boys. Right now there's not enough time. I have to hurry."

"Ahhh," the boys complained.

"Hey, if you're good all year, next Christmas I'll take you for a ride high over Slatetown. What do you think?"

Wide-eyed at this prospect, they promised they'd be extra good.

"Maybe I could be included on that trip, Santa!" Mac put in, as Jubal set the boys back down.

"Yes, and many more such trips," Jubal promised.

Stephanie leaned close and gave Jubal another kiss. "Good-bye, Santa," she said. "God bless you." And quickly, she added, "You've got your son back, the best Christmas gift anyone could ever hope for!"

"Yes, it is … indeed, it is," Jubal replied, beaming proudly at Mac.

"And the best ever for me, too," Mac said.

"Merry Christmas, Mr. MacKenzie," Stephanie said, giving Mac a hug. "And I hope we see you and Santa again." She wished the others a very Merry Christmas too, and a good night.

Stanley took Jubal's hand and nearly shook it off, repeatedly vowing never to forget what had happened.

"I'm sorry, Stan," Tom apologized, with the boys looking on, "but we have to get Santa back to his sleigh. He has a lot of work left to do tonight."

With everyone exchanging final goodbyes, Jubal, Mac, and Tom edged out onto the porch. Kirkpatrick and Walter Gaska followed them, but Steve Dixon lagged behind. "Merry Christmas," he said to Stanley, shaking his hand. Turning to Raymond and Edward, he gave them a special promise that he would indeed return soon and show them some more magic tricks. Then, looking deeply into their mother's eyes, he said, "Merry Christmas, Stephie."

"Merry Christmas, Steve," she replied.

The officer chuckled, "Where's that mistletoe when I need it?"

Laughing, Stephanie surprised him, and her brother, by giving him a quick kiss.

From outside, Tom's deep voice boomed, "Steve, come on! Let's get a move on."

Steve said a quick good night and rushed out the door.

Stanley closed the storm door, and the family remained in the doorway to watch. He put an arm around Stephanie, pulled her close, and kissed her gently on the forehead. Raymond and Edward, who held Zigzag, huddled next to them. Outside, policemen lined both sides of the walk leading from the porch to the street. Mac, Tom and Steve escorted Jubal, Mr. Kirkpatrick, and Walter Gaska past the officers. On reaching the end of the walk, Jubal turned and waved good-bye.

"Goodbye, Santa" the boys yelled.

The family waved a final good-bye to Jubal as he and his entourage went down the darkened street towards Mr. Gaska's home.

"Thank you, Lord!" Stanley whispered, touching the crucifix on the wall, before finally closing the door for the night.

He hugged his nephews close. "I love you guys," he said. "I'm so lucky to be your uncle." And then, still somewhat dazed, he settled into his easy chair, thinking about all that had happened and how amazingly fast everything had changed for the good! *Surely*, he thought, *this is the best Christmas of all!*

Resuming their play beneath the twinkling tree, the boys chattered continuously about Santa and his surprise visit. Stephanie looked on, her heart bursting with love and affection for them. "Five more minutes," she said, "then up to bed. It's been a long night."

She sat beside her brother, on the arm of his easy chair, and he took her hand. "It's a miracle," he said. "What happened here tonight was some kind of a miracle. I'll never forget Jubal."

"Neither will I," said Stephanie. "And I know the boys won't."

Leaning closer to her, he spoke in a lowered voice, "You like that policeman, don't you?"

"Yes ... yes I do, Stan," she said in a firm voice. "He's very nice."

On hearing these words, an even greater happiness swept over Stanley. He knew that all his prayers for her had finally been answered. For this, too, he was so genuinely thankful. Tenderly, he squeezed his sister's hand.

With a sigh, Stephanie said, "Things will be different now, Stan. I know they will. You've been so understanding and patient. Thank you. Thank you for every thing."

Jubal saw the Ludlow ambulance, the driver, and attendant George Schaffer waiting for him in the driveway of one of Gaska's garages. "We had the driver park down here," Tom Watson explained, "so the boys wouldn't see the ambulance."

When they reached the vehicle, George Schaffer stepped forward, complaining, "Well, it's about time. I thought maybe you guys got lost in there or something."

Moving towards Jubal, Schaffer continued, "Okay, okay, we'll take this guy now. We know how to deal with runaway whackos who think they're Santa Claus."

Surprised and angered by the attendant's demeaning words, Mac angrily declared, "Hold on a minute, buddy! That's my father you're talking about."

Schaffer jerked back in surprise. "Father?" he said.

Steve quickly stepped between the two. Looking at the attendant and driver, he declared, "You guys aren't taking him anywhere!"

"Oh yeah, why not?" George asked.

"Because your vehicle isn't safe, Wise Guy, that's why. You've got a faulty tail light."

"Say what!" George shot back, defiantly. He and the driver quickly turned to look at the rear of the ambulance. "There's nothing wrong with our tail lights," he said. "Look! They're working fine."

Steve shook his head. "No, I'm afraid they aren't. I noticed them flickering off and on as we walked down here."

"There!" Tom Watson suddenly shouted. "They just did it again."

Turning quickly, George looked back at the ambulance, only to see the taillights working just fine. "Hey, what are you guys trying to pull here?" he said.

"Must be an electrical short," Tom declared. "That's not very safe, especially for an ambulance."

Jubal chuckled as the other police officers all agreed.

Steve put a hand on the old man's shoulder, and said, "We don't often get such a distinguished guest here in town. So I think it would be more fitting if *we* took Santa back to the hospital ... with an escort, of course."

Jubal liked the idea immediately. "Good God, Gerty!" he chirped. "That would work just fine. It would be way more fitting."

George Schaffer rolled his eyes. "Now I get it," he complained. "I see what's going on!"

A gray-haired detective stepped forward and in dead-serious tones told a patrolman, "Before this ambulance leaves here, give it a good going-over. If you find other violations, give this guy a ticket. And be sure to take your time and look it over real good."

Tom and Steve wished the two men from the hospital a Merry Christmas. Then, along with Jubal, Mac and Mr. Kirkpatrick, they got in to their patrol car and drove off, with most of the other police cars following.

George Schaffer and the ambulance driver stood angrily watching. "Man oh man," George complained. "This just takes the cake."

Chapter XXIV

The bells high within St. Stanislaus' towering stone spire heralded the approach of the 9 a.m. Mass on a glorious Christmas morning in Slatetown. Raymond and Edward, dressed and ready for church, played outside with their new football, passing and kicking it to each other up and down quiet Hickory Street.

Stephanie gave her long blond hair a final brushing, and then went into the kitchen where Stanley was finishing a cup of coffee. "I'm going to go up and check on Mom," he told her. "Then we better get going."

Stephanie put on her coat and stepped out onto the front porch, surprised to see Steve Dixon, in civilian clothes, zooming past on a skateboard. She laughed with the boys when he lost his balance and tumbled over.

"Hey, are you trying to break your neck?" she called to him.

"No way," said Steve, getting up and dusting himself off. "Believe it or not, I used to be pretty good at this. I think the sidewalk is a little too rough here."

Edward quickly grabbed the skateboard, and with his brother, they skated off together, laughing.

Stephanie teased him a bit. "It's not too rough for the boys. They seem to be doing okay." She joined him on the sidewalk.

"Well," Steve laughed, watching them. "What can I say? I'm out of practice."

And suddenly thinking of something, she asked him, "Skateboards! Where in the world did they get them? Theirs are broken!"

Steve spoke up. "Last night in all the commotion, I thought I heard them say they didn't get skateboards for Christmas. So, being an ex-skate rat, I brought them a couple of mine. It's not like I'm using them anymore."

"Oh that's so sweet of you, Steve," Stephanie said. "Thank you! I'm sure the boys were so happy to get them."

Steve smiled. And for a moment the two watched the boys skate.

"Is that why you came by this morning?" Stephanie asked.

"Well, yeah," he stammered. "And I was going to Mass at St. Stanislaus and I just thought you might be going too, and, you know, maybe we could go together."

Her smile broadened. "That would be nice. Would you like to stay for breakfast after Mass?"

"I sure would! Thank you!"

As they walked back to the porch, she asked him, "How did you ever guess we were going to the nine o'clock Mass?"

"Oh, just a hunch."

"You didn't happen to hear me mention it to Mr. Gaska last night, did you?" She looked questioningly into his eyes.

Grinning, Steve replied, "Me? No way. Like I said, it was just a hunch, a policeman's lucky hunch."

Stephanie laughed. "Well I'm glad you're so lucky, and I'm glad you came by."

Stanley was surprised to find his mother in her robe and sitting up on the edge of her bed when he entered her room.

"Mom, you're up!" he said. "Are you okay? Is everything all right?"

She nodded and patted the bed next to her for him to sit. "I'm fine, Stanley," she said in her Polish accent. "Sit here. I want to tell you something."

Stanley sat beside his mother, and she took his hand in hers.

"Some weeks ago," she began, "I heard you complaining that your plant was closing and you were losing your job. It was very upsetting."

Stanley winced. "It's nothing for you to worry about, Mom. It's
..."

"Be still!" she interrupted. "Let me finish." After a pause, she
squeezed his hand gently, and continued, "Don't ever act that way
again, Stan. Never lose faith in God, or in yourself. Your father
never did. He brought us here with nothing, and we made a new
life. Losing your job is bad, but it's not the end of the world. God
will provide. And remember, this is America!"

"I'm sorry," Stanley apologized. He paused for a moment before
going on in a more confident tone. "But things are already getting
better, much better. I've got a good job offer and now, thanks be to
God, Stephanie is coming to grips with her loss. She's starting to
move on with her life."

"This is good," the old woman said, smiling and squeezing
Stanley's hand again. "This is good."

"It's very good," Stanley agreed.

"This morning I woke up to the bright sunshine, feeling its
warmth, and feeling so much better than I have in weeks."

"You're coming around, Mom," Stanley said, smiling. "You'll
be back to your old self in no time."

"I hope so, but don't forget what I said, you must never lose
faith. Never!"

"I won't, Mom, and thank you!" Stanley said. He hugged her
close and softly kissed her cheek.

For as far back as he could remember, she had always given
him good, common sense advice, and he knew she had done so
again.

The walk to church was a leisurely, pleasant one. Raymond and
Edward, staying ahead of the adults, cheerfully wished each
neighbor they met a Merry Christmas.

Stephanie and Steve talked about the events of last night.
Although Stanley walked with them, his thoughts were on the
pleasant surprise his mother had given him moments earlier. His
reflections were cut short, however, when they came upon
Raymond and Edward talking with a splendid-looking, fully
outfitted Santa Claus who had just come out of a corner house with
an armload of wrapped presents.

Dennis D. Skirvin

"Merry Christmas, Merry Christmas!" the youngsters shouted.

"Thank you, boys!" said the Santa Claus, with a heavy Polish accent. He was putting the presents into the back of a pickup truck. "A Merry Christmas to you, and God bless you both." He smiled at Stanley and the others, and exchanged Christmas greetings with them also. At Stanley's prodding, the little group continued on, but had only gone a few steps when Edward ran back to the Santa, tugged on his coat, and declared, "You're not the real Santa Claus!"

With the eyes of the others upon him, the man laughed: "No, I'm not, my little one. The real Santa Claus is back at the North Pole by now. I'm just one of his helpers, but I look just like him."

Edward, after thinking for a moment, said, "No you don't. The real Santa Claus is a jolly old black man. And I know because I met him last night!"

Edward marched off, leaving the man scratching his head. Everyone laughed, and then they all continued on.

Nearing the church, Steve took Stephanie by the arm, and confided, "You know, Stephie, maybe I shouldn't mention this so soon, but something about you hit me the moment I first saw you. I'm sure glad we met."

She smiled and nodded. "So am I."

"And there's something else." He paused for a moment before going on to admit something very personal. "You know that crazy Vietnam War robbed me of something, too. It took a big piece of my heart and froze it up solid. But meeting you ..." Choking with emotion, he left the sentence undone. In a moment, however, he added, "I'm so glad that I was with you and your family last night to share all that happened. God brought that special old man to your home to finally reunite with his son, and to help your family through a very tough time. And he brought us together for a reason, too. I'm sure of it."

Stephanie smiled. "I'm sure of it, too."

To the sound of the joyous bells, they climbed the church steps together, hand in hand, reflecting in silence. Once inside St. Stanislaus Church, they all prayed in joyful thanksgiving. Filled with the holy spirit of Christmas, Stanley Wisniewski prayed with sincere gratitude, thanking the Lord for His many blessings.

EPILOGUE

One month later.

The Friday lunch crowd at Zajack's Tavern had already thinned out when the owner came out of the back room looking unusually crisp and clean in a suit and tie and smelling of aftershave.

"Well I'll be!" called Tomasz, one of the regulars, a railroad worker in dirty jeans and sweatshirt. "Would you take a look at old Jack! Don't he look special." The man, one of a dozen or so customers in the bar, laughed good-naturedly. It was quite rare for them, or any one for that matter, to see Jack so dressed up.

The other patrons looked up to see him preening in a mirror behind the bar, and repeatedly running a hand over his cowlick in a fruitless effort to coax it to lie down. Some of the men laughed, one even whistled, while others just stared in amazement. Even Sophie, the big barmaid, chuckled.

"Go ahead, have your fun," Jack said, trying to ignore the hecklers.

"You sure you're not going to the White House, Jack?' the burly Tomasz called with a laugh.

Larry, another regular, said, "He looks spiffy enough,"

"Ok, ok, knock it off," Jack complained, giving up on his tenacious cowlick. "You guys all know where I'm going. And I'm running late, so I don't need any razzing."

"Give the mayor our best," Tomasz called to him. "And while you've got his ear, ask him to lower our taxes." The patrons laughed again.

A uniformed limo driver suddenly stepped inside the tavern, and asked, "Is there a Mr. Zajack here?"

Jack shouted, "Right here, buddy!"

"The car's outside, Sir."

"Ok, be with you in a minute," Jack assured him.

With a nod of his head, the driver turned and went back outside. Jack gave himself a final check in the mirror and one last straightening of his tie. Under the watchful eyes of his customers, he pulled on his overcoat, said goodbye to Sophie, and headed for the door.

Outside a black limousine waited next to the curb. The driver held the door for him, and feeling like royalty, Jack quickly got into the classy vehicle and marveled at the plush interior. In quick order, the driver was back behind the wheel and heading for his next stop, 408 Hickory Street.

"Sure nice of the mayor to send this limo," Jack said to the driver.

"Yes, sir," the driver replied. "It's quite the occasion."

Jack saw the Wisniewski family, including Mrs. Wisniewski, all in their Sunday best clothes, waiting on the porch as the driver pulled in front of their home. Mr. Gaska was with them, too, bundled like an Eskimo in his big, hooded overcoat. The driver dutifully got out and held the door for his riders. From nearby doorways and porches, curious neighbors watched. Some even clapped and cheered. Stanley helped his mother into the car, then Stephanie and her boys got in. Stanley and Walter Gaska followed them.

"Wow, this is really some car!" Raymond said once inside.

"Really neat!" Edward agreed, equally impressed with the limousine.

Stanley greeted Zajack, and then said, "I bet it feels funny being away from your tavern in the middle of the day."

"Oh yeah," Jack replied, nodding his head. "It sure does." And to Stanley's mother, he said, "I'm so glad that you could make it, Mrs. Wisniewski."

"Wild horses couldn't keep me away!" the old woman said. "I've heard all about the miracle that happened at our house on

Christmas Eve." And with a little laugh, she added, "It's about all I've heard ever since."

"Little wonder," Zajack said. "It's not every day a genuine, honest-to-goodness miracle happens in your home."

"You're right about that, Mr. Zajack," Stephanie said. "And we're all glad that Mom could make it." She smiled at her mother.

Zajack chuckled. "Yes indeed! This is a big day."

"It sure is," Stanley agreed.

"A very big day," Walter Gaska added.

The limousine driver exited the heavy afternoon traffic and parked in front of City Hall. Quickly getting out, he opened the door and stood erect as his passengers emerged one after another, each thanking him for the ride. Raymond and Edward stared in awe at the man, and it wasn't until Stephanie coaxed them away from him that they moved along.

"Wow!" Raymond shouted. "Look at the building."

"Yeah, and all the steps," Edward said. "Is that City Hall, Mom?"

"Yes, dear."

"We're going in there?"

"Yes. Now come on, and watch your step."

"Wow!" Raymond shouted again. The two boys broke away from their mother and raced up the steps leading to the large, ornate building. Stephanie and Mrs. Wisniewski called to them to stop, but they kept going, and were waiting at the top when they arrived.

When the group entered the sprawling lobby, Mac MacKenzie stepped forward to greet them. He shook hands with Stanley, and smiling warmly, gave them all a friendly hello. "You're right on time!" he said, looking at his watch.

"That driver was a real pro," Walter Gaska pointed out. "He knew all the shortcuts."

"Good," said Mac.

Stanley, expecting to see Jubal, asked, "Where is your father?"

"He'll be here," Mac assured him. "Now, if everyone would please follow me."

Stanley and the others fell in behind Mac as he led them through the lobby, past an area that was still being renovated, and on to the spot where the Ludlow plaque once proudly hung. Waiting for them were Tom Watson and Steve Dixon, both in their police uniforms. Mr. Michael Kirkpatrick was there with his wife, Bernadette, and Maisy Cunningham, his secretary. Dr. John Stoddard, the director of the Ludlow Psychiatric Hospital, appeared in his trademark wrinkled dark suit with Dr. Julia Nichols. A gaggle of reporters and photographers milled about the area impatiently. A group of enthusiastic 'restore-the-plaque' supporters stood by, too, along with members of the general public. In addition, some curious workmen had meandered over to see what was going on.

Mr. Kirkpatrick welcomed Stanley, his family, Mr. Gaska, and Mr. Zajack. Then he introduced his wife and Ms. Cunningham. He had just finished when Beverly Swanson, of Mayor Rocco's office, suddenly approached the gathering, and called out, "If I could please have everyone's attention." Waiting for quiet, she casually straightened her smart red skirt and matching jacket.

Mac quickly joined her.

"Hi, Bev," he said, taking her hand and giving her a quick kiss.

"Mac," she protested with a half smile. "I'm working."

Grinning, he replied, "You look beautiful!"

She blushed. Then getting back to business, she shouted to the noisy gathering once again. "Please, everyone, if I could have your attention."

Finally, all but Raymond and Edward stopped chattering, and Stephanie quickly hushed them.

"Thank you! My name is Beverly Swanson. I work for Mayor Ted Rocco, and on his behalf, I welcome each of you to City Hall and thank you for coming. This is quite an occasion. We'll get started as soon as the mayor arrives, which should be any minute. I'm going to ask you to stay right where you are. So please don't walk off." She turned to Mac, but suddenly remembered something. "Oh, pardon me," she said to the group. "Does anyone have any questions about the ceremony?"

Stanley quickly raised his hand.

"Yes, Mr. Wisniewski."

"You won't start without Mr. Flowers, will you?"

By now, only Raymond and Edward didn't know the true identity of the Santa Claus who visited them on Christmas Eve.

"I should say not," she assured him. "Mr. Flowers is our guest of honor. Now, are there any other questions?" When no one spoke up, she added, "Good. It's pretty straightforward what we're about to do."

Stanley looked around anxiously hoping to see Jubal. When the mayor arrived a few minutes later, the old man had still not appeared, and Stanley grew even more worried.

The news reporters, photographers and videographers moved forward as Mayor Rocco and an entourage of city officials took center stage. The mayor introduced himself and the other officials, and then went on to praise his own administration for the beautiful renovations being made to City Hall. He concluded by saying, "It's unfortunate that some of the work is still going on, but we won't let that diminish this celebration. Not one bit!" The cheerful crowd applauded.

Stanley leaned close to Stephanie, and said, "Where's Jubal? He should be here."

"He'll be here," she replied, sounding certain. "Don't worry."

Mayor Rocco continued, "I'm sure everyone is well aware of the happy events that took place this past Christmas Eve over in Slatetown, and how they've had a huge bearing on my decision to restore the Ludlow plaque to its former place of honor. In hindsight, the plaque never should have been removed in the first place. But, that's all behind us now. So, before I give our workmen the signal to begin ..."

Stanley suddenly raised his hand and, shouted, "Where is Mr. Flowers? You can't start without him!"

Thrown off by the interruption, the mayor looked at Stanley for a moment, then said, "I was just about to get to that Mr. Wisniewski. Now, most unfortunately, I have some bad news. Mr. Flowers had to cancel out at the last minute."

A rumble of disappointment rippled through the crowd. Some even shouted protests, but the unexpected news knocked Stanley speechless.

When order returned, Mayor Rocco resumed, his voice swelling upward into an excited crescendo, "Although Mr. Flowers can't be here, we're very fortunate to have with us a man whom you all know and love, a man who needs no big introduction." With a theatrical wave of hand, he pivoted, and continued, "So let's give a big Wilberton welcome to the one and only Santa Claus!"

Jubal Flowers, in red sports coat and fur trimmed Santa Claus hat, stepped out from behind a fork truck parked nearby in an area cordoned off for construction equipment. Recognizing him immediately, the crowd erupted in applause, including Mayor Rocco and the other officials. The representatives of the media rushed forward, snapping photos, videotaping and shouting questions. Bev Swanson quickly intervened and managed to get the disorderly herd under some control.

"It's Santa Claus!" Edward shouted excitedly.

"Yeah, it's him," his brother exclaimed. "It's him!"

The boys, who had not seen Jubal since Christmas Eve, rushed to his side, clinging to him and tugging on his red coat.

"Santa, Santa!" they cried.

Jubal's white beard seemed to sparkle in the photographers' flashing lights. He hoisted the boys up into his arms, laughing and hugging them close. Everyone clapped and cheered, while Mac joined his father and stood at his side, beaming proudly.

Mr. Kirkpatrick broke off clapping long enough to say to his wife and secretary, "This time, we *gave* him the hat and coat!"

Dr. Stoddard, applauding too, leaned toward Dr. Nichols. "So wonderfully touching!" he observed. "The entire incident ... so touching!"

"Yes it is," she replied. "Quite remarkable."

After a moment, Stoddard added, "I understand he's living with his son now."

"Yes, and that helped expedite his discharge."

With a smile, Dr. Stoddard nodded. "Wonderful."

"He's got a job, too!"

"Oh really?" Stoddard said, in surprise.

"Yes, he's working for Mr. Kirkpatrick as a watchman in his department store!"

Stoddard couldn't help chuckling. "Well how about that, a watchman in Kirkpatrick's store. What an astonishing turn of events. And to think it all started at our hospital."

Dr. Nichols turned to face the director. "I don't think we can lay claim to that, Dr. Stoddard," she disagreed.

"Oh no?" he responded in surprise.

"No, I think that honor belongs to Mr. Ludlow, on that snowy Christmas Eve of long ago."

Jubal's Christmas Gift

Realizing his error, Stoddard smiled. "Oh yes, of course. The honor belongs to Mr. Ludlow, for his impressive life of doing good for others."

Suddenly, Jubal shouted to Mayor Rocco, who was busy talking with a reporter, "Good God, Gerty! Mr. Mayor, let's get a move on. We want to hang this plaque before another Christmas rolls around!"

His words drew laughter from the crowd, and proved to be the catalyst that got the ball rolling. Mayor Rocco led Raymond and Edward up the steps leading to a wooden platform, where two workmen waited with the plaque at the ready. Mac walked alongside Jubal, carefully assisting him up the steps.

The mayor, now with a microphone in hand, followed them up and addressed the growing crowd. "Ladies and gentlemen, without any further delay, it's time to put Mr. Ludlow's plaque back where it belongs, to serve as a genuine inspiration throughout the years, most especially at Christmas time, to everyone in this great city, state and country."

He signaled the workmen to begin, and quickly prodded Jubal, Raymond and Edward to join them. Now, with the three special assistants, the workmen lifted the refurbished bronze plaque and, after a little difficulty maneuvering it into position, soon hung it on the marbled wall. As they all stepped back to admire it, the onlookers applauded and cheered. Mac hugged his father, and kissed him on the cheek. "I love you, Dad!" he said.

"I love you too, Billy!" the old man replied, with a broad, Santa Claus smile and a twinkle in his eye. "More than you will ever know. I'm so thankful we found each other."

Raymond and Edward crowded in and hugged Santa, too.

Stanley and his mother, Tom, Steve, Stephanie, Mr. Kirkpatrick, and Walter Gaska, all looked on approvingly, clapping cheerfully with the others. Mayor Rocco congratulated Jubal, then took hold of his hand, and raised it up high, causing everyone to applaud even louder.

Caught up in the excitement, Steve Dixon pulled Stephanie close and kissed her, and to his delight, she kissed him back.

Mayor Rocco raised a hand and called for quiet. It took some time and additional prodding, but when everyone finally complied, he nodded to the boys, saying, "Ok!"

With all eyes on them, Raymond and Edward shifted nervously, then stood beneath the plaque. Mayor Rocco coaxed them again, "Go ahead. Go on!"

He lowered the microphone for the boys, and very bravely, they began reading the inscription on the plaque: "Good deeds are investments in the general welfare. Properly made, they will pay dividends for years."

"Amen!" Jubal shouted, amid another outburst of clapping, cheering and the photographers' flashing lights.

"Amen!" Stanley Wisniewski shouted too, looking up at Jubal with love and admiration.

Beverly Swanson hurried up onto the platform and joined Mac and Jubal. The young man pulled them close and held them tightly, as if he'd never let them go.

Stanley felt as if his heart would burst with joy. With his precious family close to him, he silently thanked God for them, and for His many other blessings. And he gave special thanks for the miracle of Jubal's Christmas gift.

— THE END —

Made in the USA
Middletown, DE
24 November 2021

52649861R00076